Teased

ALSO FROM REBECCA ZANETTI

Teased

A Dark Protectors Novella

By Rebecca Zanetti

1001 Dark Nights

EVIL EYE

CONCEPTS

Teased
A Dark Protectors Novella
By Rebecca Zanetti

Copyright 2015 Rebecca Zanetti
ISBN: 978-1-940887-73-9

Foreword: Copyright 2014 M. J. Rose

Published by Evil Eye Concepts, Incorporated

ACKNOWLEDGMENTS

I am truly thrilled to be included with the amazing authors in the 1001 Dark Nights group! Liz Berry combined a love of reading and a brilliance for business in this exciting venture, and I'm excited to be part of the fun. I'm also honored to call her a friend, and I can't thank her enough for the good talks, ingenious ideas, and phenomenal work. Thank you also to MJ Rose, Kimberly Guidroz, and Pam Jamison for their dedication and awesome insights. A huge shout-out goes to Jillian Stein, the most amazing social media manager in the world, and the woman who has greatly reduced my stress level. Thanks also to Asha Hossain, who creates absolutely fantastic book covers.

Next I need to thank Alicia Condon and Kensington Publishing for helping me create and grow the Dark Protector world and fan base, as well as for being so supportive with my branching out a little with the series. My next shout-out goes to Caitlin Blasdell and Liza Dawson, my insightful and very hard working agents, whom I appreciate so much.

As always, a big and heartfelt thank you goes to Big Tone, my own six-and-a-half feet tall grumpy badass Alpha male. The man takes care of things, even during a recent unexpected natural disaster, and I can't express how secure this makes me. Thanks also to Gabe and Karly, our terrific kids, who definitely keep things interesting, and who I love dearly.

Finally, thank you to Rebecca's Rebels, my Facebook street team, who have been so generous with their time and friendship. And last, but not least, thank you to all of my readers who spend time with my characters.

~ RAZ

Sign up for the 1001 Dark Nights Newsletter
and be entered to win a Tiffany Key necklace.

There's a contest every month!

Go to www.1001DarkNights.com to subscribe.

As a bonus, all subscribers will receive a free
1001 Dark Nights story
The First Night
by Lexi Blake & M.J. Rose

One Thousand And One Dark Nights

Once upon a time, in the future…

*I was a student fascinated with stories and learning.
I studied philosophy, poetry, history, the occult, and
the art and science of love and magic. I had a vast
library at my father's home and collected thousands
of volumes of fantastic tales.*

*I learned all about ancient races and bygone
times. About myths and legends and dreams of all
people through the millennium. And the more I read
the stronger my imagination grew until I discovered
that I was able to travel into the stories... to actually
become part of them.*

*I wish I could say that I listened to my teacher
and respected my gift, as I ought to have. If I had, I
would not be telling you this tale now.
But I was foolhardy and confused, showing off
with bravery.*

*One afternoon, curious about the myth of the
Arabian Nights, I traveled back to ancient Persia to
see for myself if it was true that every day Shahryar
(Persian: شهريار, "king") married a new virgin, and then
sent yesterday's wife to be beheaded. It was written
and I had read, that by the time he met Scheherazade,
the vizier's daughter, he'd killed one thousand
women.*

Something went wrong with my efforts. I arrived in the midst of the story and somehow exchanged places with Scheherazade — a phenomena that had never occurred before and that still to this day, I cannot explain.

Now I am trapped in that ancient past. I have taken on Scheherazade's life and the only way I can protect myself and stay alive is to do what she did to protect herself and stay alive.

Every night the King calls for me and listens as I spin tales. And when the evening ends and dawn breaks, I stop at a point that leaves him breathless and yearning for more. And so the King spares my life for one more day, so that he might hear the rest of my dark tale.

As soon as I finish a story... I begin a new one... like the one that you, dear reader, have before you now.

CHAPTER ONE

Chalton Reese stepped smoothly around several women wearing Christmas garlands in lieu of clothing, ignoring their outstretched pamphlets. New York winter was setting in, and the wind was attacking the garlands, revealing way too much flesh. Street vendors hawked theater tickets to his left, and fluffy creatures from children books mingled to the right, trying to get tourists to pay for photographs.

Massive blinking billboards showing holiday sales bombarded him from all sides in a sensory overload that slapped him with an instant migraine.

He hadn't been in Times Square for nearly six decades, and that wasn't long enough. Not even close.

Yet the woman he followed hummed quietly beneath her breath, winding through the throng, a definite hop in her step. She had to be truly crazy to enjoy the crowd milling around.

He barely tolerated crazy, and he hated crowds. What he wouldn't give to be in his secluded computer control room deep in the Idaho mountains. But no. When the king of the Realm ordered a vampire on a mission, a vamp went on a mission. Even if that guy hadn't been on a mission in a century.

He hadn't been away from his computers for decades. Like most vampires, he employed logic and order...and couldn't for the life of him figure out why Dage had sent him on this mission. But the king always had reasons, and he usually kept them close to his vest.

Chalton stepped over a pile of what appeared to be chilidogs and hastened his step to keep the woman in sight. Olivia Roberts. A no-nonsense name with just a bit of softness. Unlike the woman. She was *all* soft and curves. Deep brown hair, light green eyes, and a figure that could literally stop a trolley cart.

He'd always liked curvy, and the beauty in front of him was overflowing with curves. Once again, he frowned, and a hot dog vendor jumped out of his way, fear sizzling from him. Chalton shook his head and tried to force his face into harmless lines. The last mission he'd been on had involved firing from a distance. Most of his missions had included guns, shooting, and death. But he'd given up the life of an assassin to become a computer geek.

Yet here he was in bone-chilling cold, surrounded by cement and glass, chasing a woman who filled out her blue parka like he'd drawn her on a notepad. Perfectly.

She clip-clopped on surprisingly high-heeled boots down a cross street, easily winding between people and stepping too close to moving vehicles. He calmly followed her, pleased to be finally getting somewhere. After watching her for two days just write news articles in her apartment, he'd started to wonder if she'd ever meet her mysterious source in person. He needed to find out who was feeding her information.

A dark van pulled up next to her, its windows blackened out. The side door slid open.

Hell. Chalton burst into a run.

A man wearing a ski mask reached out, yanked her inside, and shut the door before she could let out a scream. The van jerked to the right, horn honking, inching through the traffic.

Chalton reached it and grabbed for the door handle. Metal scratched his palm and cut deep. Bugger. It was locked. The rusty metal ripped away from the door, and he threw it to the ground.

The van veered away from him, hopped the opposite curb, and careened down the sidewalk. Bystanders yelled and jumped out of the way, spraying snow. A display of holiday T-shirts flew up in the air and crashed down in the middle of the street. The van continued on, horn blaring. Chalton jumped over a downed bicycle and ran after the careening vehicle, measuring the distance between it and the four-way stop up ahead along with the probability of an accident if the driver ran a red light.

He calculated the timing of the street light signals, catching view of a yellow light up ahead. Yep. It'd be red soon, and the van would run it. The woman probably wasn't wearing a seatbelt. The van was older and weighed around six thousand pounds. It'd withstand an accident, but without a seatbelt, Olivia might get injured. He couldn't let her get injured before he discovered her source.

Besides, after keeping an eye on her for a few days, he felt an odd sense of responsibility for her. The pretty brunette wouldn't become harmed on his watch.

The van scraped against a brick building and sparks flew. People scrambled out of the way, throwing purses and shopping bags, dodging into the street. Horns blared, and vehicles screeched to stops.

He kept his heart rate slow and his mind sharp, maneuvering around frantic people while keeping pace with the van. Two cabs collided in front of the van, careening through ice, no doubt trying to get out of the way. The driver of the van hit the brakes, but it was going too fast and impacted the yellow taxis with a loud crunch of metal on metal.

One taxi driver jumped out of his cab, swearing loudly and rounding his car.

Chalton ran in front of the guy and grabbed for the van driver's front door. Locked. The window was shaded so heavily he couldn't see in, but the hair on the back of his neck rose. It wasn't the first time he'd been in the cross hairs of a gun.

A muffled scream came from inside. Olivia.

He jumped up on the hood of the van, ignoring the hiss of steam coming from the engine. The front window was dark but not as dark as the sides. A shorter man sat in the driver's seat with a SIG pointed straight at Chalton.

* * * *

Panic threatened to consume her, so she struck out. Olivia struggled against her captor and yanked off his ski mask, her nails scraping down his face.

"Bitch," he yelped, slapping her across the cheek.

Pain exploded beneath her cheekbone. Her ears rang and she scrambled away from him. Sirens sounded in the distance, giving her hope. She leaned to the side to see the driver of the van pointing a gun out the front windshield.

A man crouched on the hood, gaze on the gun.

She shivered.

No fear showed on the guy's hard-cut face. No emotion

whatsoever. Black eyes seemed merely curious as he and the driver played some weird game of chicken. But she could almost feel the driver's stress and could definitely smell his body odor.

"Um, there's nowhere to go," she whispered as the trill of sirens came closer.

The guy in the backseat reached over and grabbed her hair, pulling back her head. Pain lanced down her scalp, and she hissed. "What do you want with me?" she muttered.

"Who's your source?" the driver asked.

She blinked. Her source? Chills cascaded down her back. "I don't know."

The hand in her hair yanked, and she cried out, her eyes watering from the pain.

The man outside the car switched his gaze to her, and she felt the impact of those eyes through her entire body. He lifted an eyebrow.

What the hell? He had a gun pointed at him, there was pandemonium all around, and he seemed mildly interested. Who was the bystander? Was he some undercover cop?

"Shoot him," the guy holding her ordered.

Her eyes widened, and she opened her mouth to yell a warning. Before she could get out a sound, the guy on the hood punched through the glass. Shards sprayed along with red. Blood.

She screamed and tried to duck away from flying glass.

The punch was so powerful the guy kept coming, one hand swiping the gun out of the way and the other snaking around the driver's neck. The driver screamed and wrapped both hands around the guy's arm, flopping like a beached fish.

Olivia yanked her head free, turned, and plowed her fist into the other guy's nose. Cartilage crunched. He howled and grabbed his face, fury darkening his eyes. She scrambled back, reaching for the door handle and kicking out. Her boot tip caught the guy under the chin, throwing back his head.

Her fingers scrambled along the handle and she jerked, sliding door open and falling backward. Her arms flailing, she managed to kick her kidnapper once again as he lunged for her before her ass hit the pavement. Water from a puddle splashed over her legs.

Pain vibrated up her spine.

Her mind fuzzing and her heart beating so fast her throat clogged, she scampered to her feet and stumbled away from the van. The guy she'd kicked shoved free just in time for the blond guy to finish with the driver, grab the doorjamb, and swing his legs around. Both knees clamped onto the guy's neck and twisted, throwing him to land on the snow covered pavement.

Olivia stilled, her gaze meeting her savior's as he landed on his feet, facing her.

Except he didn't look like a savior. Standing next to the van, his size became apparent. Well over six-feet tall, muscled and tight, with blond hair tied at the nape, he looked like an avenging...what? Not an angel. Definitely not an angel. He wore black slacks and an expensive looking button-down shirt with the sleeves rolled up. One arm dripped blood from deep scratches, and he didn't seem to notice.

The crowd milled around, some passing by, some glancing into the van.

But nobody existed except for the man. His face was an intriguing blend of hard angles: prominent jawline, slashes for cheekbones, high brows. Handsome in a too-sharp-to-be-real look. But those eyes...intelligent and knowing.

She swallowed. There was no doubt he was allowing her to look her fill. Waiting and...*allowing*.

What in the world?

She breathed out, trying to slow her heart rate. Then her brain kicked back into gear, so she turned on a heel and ran.

She tripped over a dog that scurried beneath a cart peddling roasting chestnuts. Run. She had to run. Sirens came from too far away, and she knew, somehow she just knew, that the blond guy wouldn't let her talk to the cops.

Her initial assessment about him was wrong because he couldn't be a cop. Not once had he identified himself, and he didn't seem to have a badge or a gun. In fact, a cop probably wouldn't have knocked out both men without at least trying to gain their cooperation.

The blond didn't care about cooperation.

She hurried across the street to the now moving throng of shoppers, her instincts humming. Keeping her balance, she turned slightly to look behind her. Panic rippled through her instantly.

He stalked her, calmly, easily winding through the mass of people. No tension showed on his face or in his movements. He could be out for a nice stroll through the neighborhood.

Except for his eyes. Focus, intense and absolute, lived in those dark orbs. He tracked her, keeping pace, not seeming to notice that people naturally got out of his way.

Or maybe he did notice and just didn't care.

She turned back around, her shoulders hunched. Escape. Where the hell could she go?

Pushing past a group of teenagers holding shopping bags, she edged in front of them to block her from behind. Then she dodged into a large department store and headed for the back, past all the holiday dishes.

She'd learned early on in life to listen to her instincts, and right now, they were screeching at her to get away from the man.

So she loped into a jog, careful not to trip in her favorite boots, and turned up the escalator, the toes of her shoes touching down briefly on each step. Reaching the top, she hustled through the lingerie department and ran smack into a saleswoman. Bras of every color went flying.

"Oh my. I'm so sorry." Olivia reached out to steady the girl, who appeared to be around nineteen.

The girl laughed and shoved back bright purple hair. "Are you all right?"

"No." Olivia glanced around and took several deep breaths. She should probably call the police now that she was safe.

A hand banded around her elbow in instant heat. "She had a scare outside and needs some water." The voice was smooth, cultured, and commanding.

The salesgirl blinked and stepped back, her eyes widening right before her smile followed suit. "Hello." She coughed and then pushed out her boobs under a nice silk shirt that matched her hair. "I'll, ah, get water." Turning on a sparkly wedge, she stepped over abandoned bras to head through a doorway behind the cash register.

Olivia slowly turned around and then tilted her head back...way back. The blond stared down. "Who are you?" she hissed.

"Let's go." He pulled her toward the aisle, having rolled down his shirt sleeves. Probably to cover the blood.

"No." She jerked back, not surprised when his hold didn't relent. "Release me, or I'll start screaming." That sounded like a good idea anyway. She sucked in air.

The world spun.

Somehow, she ended up with her back against a brick column and her front plastered against an impossibly hard male body. Panic engulfed her, and she opened her mouth to scream.

His mouth planted against hers, driving all sound back down her throat. A warm palm cradled her head, her whole head, and held her in place. She stilled. Completely.

Her eyes widened just as his narrowed.

Heat spread from him, all but surrounding her. The look in his eyes captured her attention as it quickly spread from determined to something...else. Something hungry.

Not once in her life had she been called dainty, but with his large frame blocking her, she felt small. Feminine. And somehow, from the interest in his eyes, powerful.

"Get your mouth off mine," she murmured against his very warm lips, her body shocked into holding still.

One of his eyebrows, much darker than his hair, arched. "Are you going to scream?" he whispered right back, the movement of his mouth against hers sending irresponsible tingles down her torso.

"Probably." Yeah. She kind of liked her lips moving against his.

He grinned. Right against her mouth, he smiled, and the tingles turned to tidal waves.

What was *wrong* with her?

She blinked.

He growled low. *Growled.*

She trembled, and some of it might have been from fear.

He levered back, his face still only an inch from hers. "Turn on that sexy heel and come with me now, or I will toss you over my shoulder and we go. Either way...we go."

She leaned back into the brick, studying his face. No humor...no give. He meant every word. While she wanted to be a badass warrior, she'd already seen him move and fight. She wouldn't win. And now she had the young salesgirl to worry about. Would he hurt her?

Olivia couldn't take the risk. "Fine." The second she was outside, she'd make a break for it. No matter how tough the guy, a good kick to the nards would take him out. Probably.

He slid his hand down her shoulder and clasped her elbow, setting her slightly in front of him and propelling her toward the down escalator. She allowed him to maneuver her but kept her shoulders back and her head up. They rode down, and tension vibrated down her back.

She tried to look agreeable as they wound through the store and exited outside to the gray and snow-falling day.

Then she turned and shot her knee up as fast as she could.

CHAPTER TWO

Chalton shifted his hips in order to deflect the female's knee and yet allow her to keep her balance. Her pretty emerald eyes had given more than ample warning of the strike coming.

She huffed and set her leg back down.

"You done?" he asked mildly.

A wild, very wild, flush worked its way up over her neck, chin, and high cheekbones. "Not even close."

Damn, he liked that spirit. Liked it a whole lot. "That's unfortunate." He glanced around at the mass of bodies rushing past them living lives he truly didn't care about. "Olivia, we need to talk."

She tried to step back, and he grasped her hand to keep her from being swept away. "How do you know my name?" All color drained from her pretty face.

He cocked his head to the side. "I've been following you for two days."

Her pointed chin lifted. "I haven't gone anywhere for two days."

"I know. It's been very boring." But now she was in his hands, and he could finish his mission. Although threatening her to keep quiet and stop writing about his people didn't seem so clear-cut now that he'd had his mouth on hers. On her very heated, soft, feminine mouth. His gaze dropped on its own volition to those plump lips.

She cleared her throat. "Stop looking at me like that."

He lifted his head. "Like what?"

She licked her lips, and he groaned out loud. "What do you want, buddy?"

He grinned. "Chalton. My name."

"Chalton." She rolled the sound around on her tongue.

Now he fucking loved his name. "Yeah."

"Russian?"

"A long time ago." About three centuries, to be exact.

"You don't have an accent." Suspicion darkened her eyes to the color of a green sapphire he'd seen once in a royal crown.

"Я хочу, чтобы лишить вас голым."

"Hmm." Her shoulders settled, as she no doubt found some measure of safety with people all around them. "What did you say?"

He couldn't repeat what he said since it involved getting her naked and was no doubt very inappropriate. "I wished you a good day."

"Right. What do you want?" Clearly, she didn't believe a word he said.

"To talk." He glanced around. "Away from the crowds and the cold wind."

"Ah." She nodded, the wind lifting her hair. "In your spaceship or lair? You wanna wear my skin as a suit, do you?"

He laughed, unable to help himself.

She blinked again. "Murderous kidnappers shouldn't have such nice laughs," she murmured and then stilled.

Did the woman say everything that was in her head? While the idea should irritate him, instead he found an intriguing charm in the idea. Creative people were often the most interesting, now weren't they? "I have no plans to murder you."

"That's a relief," she snapped, trying to pull her hand free.

He kept it, quite liking it where it was in his. Then he settled. Energy cascaded around her, filtering through the air. "Ah, hell." Enhanced. The most beautiful woman he'd held in eons was enhanced and thus a possible vampire mate. Was she psychic? Empathic? Human females with special gifts were probably linked to the witches and were possible mates to immortals like him. "The king had better not be matchmaking," he muttered, losing his smile.

Olivia lifted a finely arched eyebrow. "The king? What king?"

Now he was blurting out his thoughts. "Forget it. We need privacy for a talk as well as to protect your safety. Any idea who the men in the van were?" They were human, but he hadn't had a chance to interrogate them before she'd bolted into the store, and now it was too late. The cops had arrived and were questioning people down the street.

He knew the second she caught sight of the police because her body stiffened and drew in air. "Don't do it," he said, leaning into her.

She gasped, and her head shot up, those green eyes narrowing. "Kiss me again, and you'll lose a lip."

He grinned. "Damn, you're feisty." Then he lowered his head to within an inch of hers, letting intent and focus show. "And that wasn't a kiss."

She swallowed and glanced down at his mouth before looking back up. Pink colored beneath the smooth skin on her face, and she cleared her throat. Her scent of wild flowers wafted around and tempted him far more than he liked, as did the curiosity in those stunning eyes. "Back away," she whispered.

"Promise you'll come with me and not scream." He tried to smooth his face into reassuring lines. "You have my word I won't harm you."

She snorted. "Right." Her shoulders drooping, she glanced around. "I appreciate you rescuing me from the guys in the van, but I don't know you. Or trust you."

He nodded. "I understand, but you're probably still in danger. Let's get out of here."

She shook her head. "I'll make you a deal. There's a café across the street. We can go in, have a cup, and talk. Make your case and explain why you rescued me from the van, who you are, and what you want from me." She turned back to him. "Or I start screaming my bloody head off and kicking like you've never seen a woman kick."

His groin tightened. Right there, in the middle of the sidewalk, just like a teenager...he got hard. Spunk and brains had always done him in with women, and this one had both in spades. The cops were getting closer, and there was a good chance the men in the van had friends also looking for the female. "Fine." He kept ahold of her to lead the way across the street, winding through barely moving vehicles.

Her skin was soft and her hand small. Somehow, it felt just right in his.

He shook his head. There wasn't time for this. Even as his body rioted, he could feel danger stalking near. Energy popped in the air, and his breath quickened.

Just as he reached the coffee shop door, a ping next to him threw up concrete.

Shit. Somebody had shot at them. He pivoted and shoved Olivia in front of him, propelling her to the side of the building. Covering her with his body, he glanced around the corner.

Sunlight glinted off a riflescope atop the brick building across the street. The gunman was crouched down, barely visible behind the sniper's rifle. He'd only taken one shot, and the passersby hadn't even noticed.

"What?" Olivia gasped, her back to the building.

"Sniper across the way." He looked down at her fashion boots, quickly calculating escape routes. "Can you run in those things?"

"Sniper?" She tried to lean around him and look, but he planted a hand on her upper chest and shoved her back. "You're freakin crazy."

He squinted up at the steel-structured building across from his current one-way street. If there was one killer, there might be two, and Olivia was vulnerable on the street. No movement showed across the way, but his instincts kept humming.

Going with his gut, he grabbed the door of a cab driving by and yanked it open. The driver hit his brakes, scattering slush. Chalton shoved Olivia inside before him. He sat and slammed the door.

The cab driver, a swarthy man wearing a spotted tie decorated with Rudolph, glared. "Get out. Light isn't on."

Chalton drew out several hundred-dollar bills from his pocket to hand over the seat. "Drive. Now."

The guy snatched the cash and turned to hit the gas pedal.

Olivia recovered and scooted for the other side, reaching for the door handle.

Chalton clasped her arm and dragged her into his side, giving her a warning squeeze. When she stiffened, glancing at the driver, he leaned in to whisper, "The driver can't take me, and you'll put him in definite danger if you ask for help."

She exhaled slowly, thoughts scattering across her pretty face.

"Drive faster, and I'll tip you well," Chalton spoke louder, keeping his gaze on Olivia. Who was trying to shoot her? While he'd read all of her news reports detailing the missing proprietary information from the labs his people had used to generate a cure for a virus that had attacked vampire mates, he hadn't spent any time reading her other works. "What are you involved in?" he growled.

She shivered and clasped her hands in her lap. "Bite me," she whispered back.

Hell, he'd love to bite her. A pretty woman should never say such a thing to a hungry vampire.

He leaned over her to look out her window, and she gasped, edging back in the seat. The figure on top of the building ran in pace with the taxi, rifle in hand, easily keeping up. He wore all black—including a mask. Yet there was something familiar in the way he moved.

Chalton frowned. Who the hell was that?

They needed to cross an intersection. No way could the sniper leap across the street.

Apparently the shooter realized the same thing, because he ran ahead. Probably to set up for a shot.

"At the corner, turn left suddenly," Chalton ordered the driver. "It'll be worth a thousand." He hoped he had that much in his pocket.

Olivia turned wide eyes on him. "You are batshit crazy, you know that?"

The driver shrugged and kept to the left, honking his horn several times to keep folks moving.

Bullets sprayed the side of the taxi.

"What the hell?" the driver bellowed.

Chalton yanked Olivia across his body to the other side, blocking her. She landed with a muffled *oof.*

"Oh my God. They are shooting at us," she yelled.

"Yes." Chalton glanced ahead.

She frantically patted his sides. "Shoot back."

He frowned. "I don't have a gun."

"Why the hell not?" she yelled.

"Don't like them." Not anymore. He didn't need guns. Finally, they reached the intersection. "Turn. Now."

Tires screeched as the driver turned. Chalton grabbed the back of Olivia's head and pushed her toward the floor. "Get down." Depending on the angle, the shooter might be able to make a shot through the back window.

The driver edged down in his seat, barreling through traffic. The stench of fear filled the car.

Chalton ducked down and took a good look. With his eyesight, he could make out the serial number on the rifle as well as the height of the shooter. The guy stood up, watching the cab, his gun aimed harmlessly at his feet. He stood several inches over six-feet tall, with a well-muscled form. Smooth and graceful even with such bulk.

He yanked the mask off, revealing a cap of dark hair and familiar, mocking dark eyes. Then he smiled—slow and dangerous.

Everything in Chalton stilled. His head jerked back. "Son of a bitch."

Olivia glanced up from her perch on the floor. "What? Do you know the guy?"

"Yeah." A rock settled hard in his gut. "He's my older brother."

CHAPTER THREE

Olivia planted both hands on the torn leather seat and pulled herself up. Fear tasted like acid in her throat, and an unwelcomed heat filled her lungs as a prelude to a possible panic attack. "Your brother just shot at us?"

"Apparently." Chalton eyed the festive storefronts now speeding by. "Stop at the next light and let us out," he ordered the driver.

Olivia edged toward her door that led to the busy street.

The driver, muttering beneath his breath, yanked the car to the curb. "Get out of here." He turned furious eyes toward the back seat. "I'm calling the cops."

Chalton handed over what looked like a wad of cash. "No cops." Without waiting for an answer, he clamped a hand around Olivia's arm and hastened her across the seat and out his door.

The cabbie sped off.

Olivia glanced at the top of nearby buildings. "Tell me you only have one brother."

"Two." Chalton rubbed the back of his neck. "We need cover." Keeping her arm, he led her across the sidewalk to a specialty cigar shop, quickly texting something on a type of smartphone she'd never seen before.

Olivia's ears rang and her temples began to pound. She glanced around the shop for another exit, but a glass cabinet blocked the entire rear of the store. One proprietor assisted two elderly gentlemen near the wall. No help there.

Chalton kept his gaze out the window at the people hurrying by.

"What is your plan?" Olivia asked, trying to wriggle out of his grasp.

"Hold on," he said, not moving.

The strong scent of pipe tobacco wafted around, reminding her of her grandfather, who lived in Washington state near a forest. That's where she could go for a while until things calmed down. All she had to do was escape Chalton and get on the road. Then she could figure out who wanted her dead.

His hold remained secure around her hand, easily keeping her captive. She reached for his restraining hand with her free one and dug in her nails.

He slowly turned his head and focused on her. "What?"

"Let. Go."

"No." He turned back to the window.

She dug in, making sure to draw blood. Her fingertips suddenly burned. "What the heck?"

"Move now." He opened the door and tugged her outside to where a dark town car had maneuvered to the curb. Yanking open the door, he pivoted and pushed her inside before following.

Coolness surrounded her along with the scent of expensive leather. Chalton sighed and relaxed back into the seat. Then he reached into a side cupboard for two bottled waters, handing her one.

She took the water, her heart racing. A dark partition remained up between the back and front. "Who is up there?" she asked.

"Hired driver." Chalton opened his water and tipped his head back to drink.

She rapped her knuckles against the partition and then winced. "Hey, buddy? This is kidnapping, and you're an accomplice."

"Hired driver paid really well," Chalton said smoothly.

She whirled on him, her temper finally catching up to the fear of the day. "What do you want from me?"

His dark eyes narrowed. "I want to know who your source is, where your research materials are, and where the latest article for *Life and Science* is."

"For what story?" She kept her chin up. After working for the magazine for nearly five years, she knew how to protect a source. More importantly, the only way to save her friend's life was to find the subjects of her article.

He smiled without an ounce of humor. "You know what story. The one about the laboratory in Oregon researching genetic mutations that hints at something...new."

New? Yeah. That was one way of putting it. The research hinted that there were other species walking around on earth who had more chromosomal pairs than humans. Something more...than human. Something that would certainly have a way to save Ronni from dying way too young. "I don't know what you're talking about."

He exhaled and stretched out long, very long, legs. "Sure you do. Your first two articles in the series detailed missing researchers from Oregon along with hints about their missing research, all leading up to an article coming next week with a big reveal. I'm assuming the big reveal is the actual research into chromosomal pairs, into extra ones belonging to an imaginary species, and you're being duped."

"Oh yeah?" She put her hands on her hips and pivoted in the seat to face him. "If I'm being duped, then why are people trying to either kidnap or shoot me?" She was on to the find of the century, and she needed to get back on track to meet her source for the evidence. "Let me out of this car, and I won't press charges."

"Do I look like I'm worried about charges?"

No. Not at all. He looked like some badass vigilante in tailored clothing. All muscle, intelligence, and...maleness. So damn *male* he could define the word. "You should be worried," she countered, her stomach dropping. The guy couldn't care less. She'd seen his face. She knew his name. "You're going to kill me," she whispered, her heart clenching. "Or try to," she added quickly.

He tossed his empty water bottle into a trash receptacle near the door. "I've saved your life twice. If I wanted you dead, you'd be dead."

A chill crawled down her back. "But you need the information you mentioned." Then would he kill her? Or try to?

He leaned toward her, bringing heat. "Listen, Livy. I will not kill you. I promise."

Livy? Only her grandpop called her that, and hearing the nickname from Chalton's handsome lips gave her odd tingles she really had to banish. She pressed her lips together. "Have you killed anybody before?"

"Yes."

She knew it. Of course he had. The guy was definitely a soldier from the way he moved. "In times of war?"

"Yes."

Hope unfurled inside her. "In other times?"

"We're usually at war." He shrugged. "Where's your research?"

She slowly twisted the lid open on her bottle. "At my apartment on my computer." If she could just get home, she could break free. No way did he know her neighborhood as well as she did.

"No it isn't. The only stuff on your computer is recipes, Christmas card lists, music, games, and videos. No work." He rubbed his strong jaw.

She frowned. "How do you know what's on my computer?"

"I hacked it."

Hacked it? He'd freakin hacked it? "How dare you."

He rolled his eyes. "I'm guessing you have a laptop somewhere, one with the WIFI disabled, that you use for writing. It isn't in your apartment, and you haven't gone anywhere the last two days. Where is it?"

She blinked, her throat closing. Her hand shook, but she tipped the water bottle to her mouth and drank, allowing the liquid to soothe. Finally, she drew in a deep breath. "How do you know the laptop isn't in my apartment?"

"I searched your place while you were sleeping last night." He grinned. "Love the yellow panty set with the day of the week sewn in, by the way."

She gasped.

"And," he continued, "you really shouldn't hide your grandmother's jewelry beneath the kitchen sink in an old coffee can. It's way too easy to find there."

Oh God. He'd actually been in her apartment while she'd slept. Vulnerability slammed into her chest. "You dick," she murmured.

He nodded. "If I wanted to harm you, I could have already."

Yeah, but he hadn't found the information he'd wanted, now had he? Just how deadly would he become if he got his hands on her laptop and research materials? She shuddered. "So, let me get this straight. You're a good fighter, you're drop-dead quiet at night, and you know how to hack a computer."

"I'm complex," he drawled. "The research?"

As far as she could tell, the research, or the secrecy of it, was the only thing keeping her alive. "I'm not telling you." Unfortunately, she didn't exactly possess the important documents proving the existence of this super species since her meeting had been thwarted by the guys in the van. "Why is your brother trying to kill me?" Her eyes widened. "Or was he just after you?"

"I'm thinking he was shooting toward you," Chalton said.

"Toward?"

"Yeah. If my brother wanted a bullet to impact either one of us, we'd be bleeding right now. So my thought is that he was after you, saw me, and fired for fun."

Her eyes widened. "Your brother fired at us for fun?"

"You'd have to know him." Chalton rubbed his chin. "I haven't talked to him in a long time, but—"

"Why not?"

"Huh?"

"Why haven't you talked to your brother?" she asked.

His eyes sobered. "Long story and family stuff. But if Jared is after you, it has to be connected to the Oregon lab stories."

"Why? What does your brother do besides shoot at people from rooftops?" She had to figure a way out of the car when it slowed down.

"He's for hire—a bit of a vigilante. Anybody could've hired him." Chalton shook his head. "This doesn't make sense. Who is your source for the Oregon lab series of stories?"

She clamped her mouth shut.

His chin lowered. "Listen. I don't want to scare you, and I don't want to hurt you. But I have a job to do, and I need to get a name from you."

Her mind spun. "So it's true. It's all true." Sure, she had the proof, or she would have it soon. But somehow, she'd still held doubts. "There's a species out there, or at the very least a human mutation that has created beings with more chromosomal pairs than twenty-three." More than human.

"Don't be silly." He reached out and clasped her chin with his thumb and forefinger. "My employer wants the information from the Oregon research labs because it is proprietary and could lead to drugs that'll wipe out dangerous diseases. There's no ultra-human, and you have to know that."

But the documents were clear, and she trusted Helen, her source. The woman was brilliant and knew what she was talking about. "This can't be about a simple drug."

"It's about many drugs, which means millions, if not billions, of dollars." He released her. "Give me the information, and I'll make sure you're protected. You need that."

She would be fine if she could just put some distance between herself and anybody trying to kidnap her, including Chalton. When she obtained the rest of the proof, she could finish her article and the truth would be out there, so there'd be no reason to harm her. Plus, then she could find the people who could save Ronni's heart from quitting for good. A thirty-year-old woman who'd been afflicted by an odd virus that had attacked her heart, Ronni had been Olivia's best friend since preschool. "Obviously you've read the two published articles, and you know a third is coming, so I'm not going to lie to you," Olivia said.

"Good."

"But I've already turned in the third article to my editor, and it runs next Wednesday. So it's too late." She lifted her hands.

"No you haven't," Chalton countered. "I hacked all the computers at the magazine as well as your editor's two computers at home. The guy plays way too much Zombie Bagus IV, by the way."

Her mouth dropped open. "You did not hack the magazine. We have top of the line firewalls."

"Took me almost five minutes, but I was eating a bagel at the time." He leaned in. "Maria Ortiz has pictures of her grandbabies all over her computer. Todd Jones has an affinity for sports cars, and Frank Softos likes pictures of naked softball players. Shall I go on about more of your colleagues?"

"God no." She sat back. How had he hacked the system so easily? "Who are you?"

He leaned into her space, all intent. "I'm a guy who gets the job done, no matter the job. Work with me, Livy. It's your only option."

Man, she must really be on to something with the story. Just how far did the knowledge go? The lab was a private lab, but it did have governmental funding. Was the government doing experiments? "Are you a soldier?"

"Not anymore."

She blinked. "What does that mean?"

"I used to be a soldier, a long time ago, and now I work with computers. Primarily." He glanced out the window. "I'm having men fetch your things from your apartment, including the jewelry. Is there anything you want me to make sure they pack?"

She sat back, her ears burning. "You're doing what?"

He lifted an eyebrow. "I'm taking you to a safe house and figured you'd want your things with you. On the way we need to acquire your research materials and laptop."

Oh, absolutely not. "My neighbors will report me missing, as will friends and coworkers." So would her grandfather after a few days, since they spoke at least once a week.

"I sent emails to your boss from your computer, and I left notes on your neighbors' doors in your handwriting saying you're taking a vacation. As for your grandfather, he won a two-week fishing trip in Alaska but had to leave immediately." Chalton pointed to her small purse. "There should be a message from him."

She could only gape. "Who are you?"

"I told you."

No, he really hadn't. "All I know is that you were a soldier, are probably in your early thirties, and now work as a computer hacking mercenary for hire. And you have two brothers you haven't spoken to in a while. Brothers who shoot at you."

He shrugged. "What else is there to know? Except you need to cooperate with me for your own safety, which obviously is in doubt."

"I'll be fine once I publish the next article." She spoke evenly, hoping he was truly rational.

"That will never happen." He lifted a shoulder. "Honest. You need to understand that we will take out the entire building housing the magazine in order to prevent that from happening. The whole block if we need to do so."

She studied him. Dead serious. Not an ounce of doubt showed on his hard-cut face. "You mean that."

"I truly do." He brushed a wayward hair off her forehead. "We'd try desperately to limit casualties, probably by calling in some sort of deadly gas leak and forcing an evacuation, but I can't guarantee nobody would be hurt."

The sheer calmness of his statement convinced her. "You people are zealots."

"No."

"Crazy, greedy bastards?" Heat roared into her face, burning her cheeks.

"Not really." He leaned back and stretched out again. "Look at us as folks trying to do the right thing and protect a bunch of people. From diseases and, ah, such."

Her focus narrowed. "What are you not telling me?"

He smiled, full of charm this time. "Nothing. I assure you."

Yeah, right. "I'm not telling you where my laptop is." There was no reason to deny its existence to him, considering it was obvious she'd written the articles somewhere and had the supporting documents beforehand.

"I won't make you talk." His long fingers tapped a rhythm on the leather armrest. "But you have to understand that I'll go through every aspect of your life, every friend, every acquaintance, as well as your financials, until I find the location of your hidey-hole."

She bit back a growl. "You'll never find it."

"We'll see."

The car took a sharp left and drove onto the freeway. "Where are we going?" she asked.

"The airport."

Her head jerked back. "What? Why?"

"I didn't say the safe house was in New York, now did I?"

CHAPTER FOUR

Chalton stepped from the car and held out a hand for Olivia. She completely ignored him and charged out by herself, stepping to the side and glaring at the private jet waiting on the tarmac.

"Kidnapping and transporting across state lines will land your butt in federal prison for a long time, jackwad." She pressed her hands to her curvy hips. "You could still stop this train of disaster before it ruins your life."

Those green eyes lasered into him, and his cock sprang to life. That spirit combined with obvious intelligence just turned him the hell on. "Thanks but no."

She hissed and looked around the quiet and remote hangar at the private part of the airport. "Where is everybody?"

"The pilots are in the plane and waiting. Other than that, we're the only ones close enough to hear if you start screaming. So don't." A part of him, one he didn't much like, wished she'd start fighting again just so he could put his hands on her. He wouldn't hurt her, but man, he'd like to kiss her for real. "Please embark."

Now she crossed her arms. "Screw you."

"Is that an invitation?" Ah, hell. He shouldn't have said that.

Color burst across her face, and she swung out her arms. "No. And if you think I'm meekly going to get on that plane bound for psychoville, you're fucking crazy." Her eyes sizzled, and even her lips turned an enticing rosy shade of red.

"God, you're beautiful," he murmured.

Somehow that made her even madder. "You are such a dick. Guys like you don't find girls like me beautiful." Spitting fire, she glared up at him.

He leaned into her, loving the way her eyes widened in awareness. "Guys like me?"

"Yes." She slapped both hands against his chest and shoved, snarling when he didn't move an inch. "Guys who spend hours in the gym, probably only eat protein, look like action movie stars, and probably date models who weigh three pounds."

He frowned. "What's wrong with protein?"

"Nothing," she shouted.

Somehow he'd made her so angry she'd stopped making any sense. "Your beauty isn't exactly a matter of opinion, darlin'. You're stunning."

"Stop playing with me," she almost growled.

"I haven't started playing with you, and when I do, you'll fucking know it," he shot back, rapidly losing a temper he never lost.

That apparently did it, because she levered back and kicked him square in the ankle. Pain ricocheted up his shin. Before he could respond, she pivoted and punched him right in the mouth.

"That's it." He ducked a shoulder into her stomach and lifted, easily tossing her over his shoulder.

She landed with a soft *oomph* and stilled. Then the air must've filled her lungs. "You goddamn sonuvabitch loser fuckwad hacker dickhead," she screamed, kicking out and punching his ribs with small fists.

The woman had quite a temper, now didn't she?

He turned and headed toward the plane. If she was his, he'd tuck his fingers in very inappropriate places to stop her tirade and hold her in place. As it was, he had to just wrap an arm around her legs to protect his front and allow the blows to the back to continue. "Man, you're feisty," he said.

Her response ran together so quickly he couldn't make out individual words, but he was fairly certain a death threat was in there somewhere.

He carried her right up the stairs to the plane, ducked, and dropped her ass on a leather sofa. Before she could strike out, he manacled her wrist and zip-tied it to the arm of the couch.

"What the hell?" She looked up, eyes round.

He sighed. "I can't have you jumping out, now can I?" Ignoring her furious struggles with the tie, he strode down the aisle to rap on the door and then lean in. Charlie, a feline shifter, was piloting along with a vampire copilot. "Take her to the drop, and wait for me there. Please radio for a second plane."

Charlie grinned at the swearing coming from the back. "Man, she can string words together."

Chalton nodded. "Wait until she really gets going." He shut the door and headed back toward the furious woman. "The plane ride won't be long, and the copilot will come out and cut your binding after reaching cruising altitude."

She stopped swearing and looked up at him, her eyes the green of fury. "You're not coming with me?"

His chest warmed. Even though she was pissed, did she want him with her? "I have something else to do here, but then I'll meet you. I promise."

Her glare turned even darker. "I hope you get hit by a bus."

All right, so she didn't want him with her. "I'll try." Indulging himself and knowing she'd probably bite him, he leaned down and pressed his mouth against hers. When she didn't bite, he moved, finally kissing her.

Fire lanced through him and landed in his gut. She kept still and then slowly, tentatively kissed him back. He kept the pressure light and gentle, when all he really wanted to do was push her back and go as deep as they both could take it.

Finally, he lifted his head. Her eyes had softened to the color of a spring meadow, and her lips pursed in a thoughtful O.

She leaned toward him, her gaze on his. "I'm probably going to kill you," she whispered, temper still in her tone.

He grinned. The woman had made him smile more in the last several hours than he had in many years. "Thanks for the fair warning. Here's one back. Every time you swear at me, every time you physically attack me, and definitely every time you try to kill me...I'm going to kiss you until you stop."

Her lip curled. "Then I'll just have to succeed with the kill."

Smart and spirited. "I look forward to it." Whistling, he turned on his heel and exited the plane.

A ruckus sounded from inside, and he turned just as Charlie leaned out to shut the door. "She kicked me," Charlie complained, rubbing his shin.

"She does that." Chalton chuckled and slid inside the car. It was time for a family reunion.

* * * *

Igor's smelled the same. Leather, pipe smoke, tobacco, and varnish. Different vodkas took up the shelves, and men sat around in booths or at the bar drinking. No dart boards, no pool tables, no video games. It was a bar, and bars were for drinking.

Chalton made his way to a booth at the back, not surprised to find his brother waiting. "You shot at me," he said mildly, pressing into the booth.

"I didn't hit you," Jared returned, pushing a shot of vodka from the home world his way. "I almost hit you in the leg just for fun, but I thought it might freak out the woman too much."

Chalton took the drink and downed it, enjoying the warmth spreading right to his gut. It had been over a hundred years since he'd drank with his brother, yet the moment felt like home. Was it home? He should've tried to mend fences before now, but he had struggled for so long to find himself again that he hadn't reached out. Then it became odd to reach out. "Who hired you?"

"Right to business, is it?" His brother's dark eyes glimmered in the dim light. He'd cut his long dark hair shorter so it just reached his nape, and he'd filled out even more in the century or so they'd been apart. "Your hair is long."

"Yours is shorter than normal." Even though they sat only a couple of feet from each other, the chasm felt much bigger. Grand Canyon big. Chalton reached for the bottle to pour two more shots, wanting so badly to return to normal. "No longer trying to be a pirate?"

Jared sighed. "The high seas aren't what they used to be, unfortunately."

Chalton shook his head. "I'm sure you've found many ways to rob people without a ship and dangerous weather." For years, his oldest brother had been a feared pirate on the open seas, even after the seas were somewhat tamed. Truth be told, Chalton had always liked that part of Jared. Admired it, even. "Now you're taking contracts for innocent women?"

"As are you," Jared returned, reaching for his glass. "Please tell me you're not playing the conscious here...we both know your former occupation."

"I was a soldier," Chalton said, defensiveness rising up in him.

"An assassin for the Realm," Jared said softly.

This time the liquid didn't burn quite as much. "I did my job, and I had a purpose."

Jared drank down the shot. "Being a pirate had a purpose, too. Damn, I miss those days."

Even without the long hair, Jared looked dangerous enough to be a pirate. Square jaw, broad shoulders, fighting shape. But beyond that, a wildness lived in him and always had. He'd never tried to force Chalton into his escapades, somehow understanding Chalton's need for something more than adventure.

"Those days will come back somehow and someday," Chalton said. Maybe with hovercraft or something goofy like that.

"I hope so."

"Was that Theo with you when you tried to shoot me?" Chalton asked. Had both of his brothers held him in a scope on the same day?

"Nope. Haven't talked to him since the last day I talked to you." Jared poured more vodka.

What a shitty day that was. They buried their father, had an immeasurable amount of alcohol, and had ended up battering each other bloody, saying things that never should've been said. Things none of them probably even meant. "So you haven't seen him in a century, either?"

"Nope." Jared glanced sideways. "You haven't talked to him?"

"No." Chalton scratched his neck. "I, ah, am sorry about the fight. It wasn't any of our faults that our father died."

Jared gazed at the smooth wooden table. "I should've been with him when he sought out Peter Libscombe."

"We both should've, but he didn't let us know." Instead, when their father went to challenge Peter Libscombe over a land dispute dealing with several mountain ranges, he'd taken his brother. "Uncle Jack should've called us."

"Maybe. Neither one of us would've asked for help, either." Jared kicked back in the booth. "Uncle Jack killed Peter Libscombe and survived that battle but died in the Kurjan war."

Chalton blinked. "Hell, that's true." His mother had let him know, but he'd been in the middle of planning Realm strategy during the war and hadn't reached out to his brothers...yet again. "That makes you the patriarch of the family." He chuckled, unable to help himself.

"Sounds all official and grown up, right?" Jared shook his head. "Mom's on me to find a mate and give her grandkids."

"Well, you are four centuries old." That was still young as far as

Chalton was concerned.

"You're three." Jared played idly with his shot glass.

Yeah, and he had a job to do. "Were you hired to kill Olivia, Jared?"

"No." Jared poured more drinks. "I was hired to capture her and get her to give up her source for the story about vampires existing. The gun was because I knew somebody was following her but didn't know it was you or the humans in the van."

"Who hired you?"

"Private group out of Monaco. Wealthy group of vampires with a small power base. Don't align with the Realm but don't oppose your people, either. They just want the magazine articles stopped before humans start believing it."

Chalton nodded. All immortal species vowed to keep their existence a secret. If humans knew immortality was possible, they'd never stop trying to obtain it. War with humans would be disastrous because humans would lose. Vampires were male only, and since so many human females eventually became vampire mates, the risk in losing too many of them was unacceptable. Enhanced human females, those with extra gifts like psychic or empathic abilities, could mate a vampire, shifter, demon, or witch.

He cleared his throat. "I've locked the woman down and will discover and take care of her source."

Jared eyed him. "Oh, will you?"

"Yes."

"She's a looker, isn't she?"

Chalton leaned back. "She's stunning." He twirled his glass in his hands. "And enhanced."

Jared's eyebrows shot up. "Enhanced? You thinking of settling down?"

"No." But if he were, it'd be with a sexy, curvy, brilliant smartass of a woman. Like Olivia. "Not anytime soon."

"Me either." Jared tipped over the empty vodka bottle. "So you're not claiming the woman."

"No." Heat spiraled through Chalton, and his focus narrowed. "Are you?"

"No." Jared grinned. "We're at a standstill then."

Chalton's shoulders went back. "I don't see how. I have the woman."

"Where is she?"

Now he chuckled. "I'm not telling."

"Well, then. I guess I'll have to change your mind." Faster than ever, Jared shot out the first punch.

Chalton's cheek exploded in pain, and his head jerked back. Anticipation roared through him, and he plowed a fist into his brother's nose.

It was on.

CHAPTER FIVE

Two hours. Two whole hours. Olivia had sat in the chilly private airplane hangar, cuffed to a metal chair, for two hours. The pilots were in an office, doing a bunch of stuff with maps and ignoring her.

She'd kill them.

Once she got free, and she would, she'd end them. Somehow. Okay, she didn't know how, but she'd come up with a plan. Or run. Yeah, that was it. She'd just run and call the police. Much better plan.

A loud whir echoed, and the massive hangar door opened. A jet, this one a little smaller than the one that had flown her there, rolled in. The engines cut, the door opened, and Chalton jogged down the stairs.

She gasped. Cuts and bruises marred his skin, while rips showed throughout his bloody clothing. "What happened to you?"

"Family reunion." He reached her in long strides. "Charlie?" he called out.

The pilot with reddish-blond hair stepped out of the office and lobbed a small key toward Chalton. "Have fun."

Olivia should've kicked him a few more times. She hissed, and he quickly dodged back inside the office.

"Easy," Chalton said, unlocking her cuffs. "We're in a quiet part of the very private airport, and nobody else is around. I have a car right outside, and you can choose to walk or go over my shoulder again." Then he stepped back and crossed his arms.

She leaned to look around him at two men transferring items quickly from the plane to outside. Hey. That was her suitcase. "You brought my belongings."

"Yes. I had them collected while I dealt with my brother. He won't harass you again." Chalton fingered a bruise under his left eye.

She jumped to her feet. "Oh my God. You killed your brother."

Chalton blinked, studied her, and then threw back his head and laughed. Finally, he coughed. "I did not kill Jared. We got in a fight, I knocked him out, and then I came here. He has no clue where you are, so he'll back off now. So long as our missions are the same, which they are."

She planted both hands on her hips. "Meaning making my articles disappear."

"Yes." He towered over her without even meaning to do so. "Walk or ride, baby. Make a decision because night is falling, and I'd like to get cleaned up."

It was beyond tempting to kick him again and fight, but she wouldn't win. And everybody else around there worked for him and certainly wouldn't jump in on her behalf. Even so, pride mattered. She just couldn't help it. She leaped up, punched him in the gut, turned, and ran around him.

Well, she tried to run around him.

He halted her with one arm banded around her forearm. "Jesus, Livy." Jerking her around, he ducked, and once again she found herself face down over his shoulder.

How did he do that? It wasn't like she was a hundred pound yoga instructor. Yet the guy slid into motion, easily striding across the hangar for the outside like she wasn't flopping over his shoulder like a flounder. "Let me go," she ground out, trying not to shake out her aching fist. His stomach was harder than a boulder she'd tripped over at the lake last summer.

Cool air brushed across her legs as they exited the hangar, the world tilted, and she found herself in the front seat of a dark SUV. Chalton leaned over her, his handsome face within an inch of hers, snow dotting his hair. "Do I need to tie you to the seat?"

Heat and male...so damn much heat and male. Her gaze dropped to his lips, and swear to God, everything inside her turned mushy. How could this be happening? No way, no way, was she attracted to a kidnapper. "Stockholm syndrome," she murmured.

He smiled, those gorgeous lips moving. "Keep telling yourself that."

Her gaze slashed up to his to see those dark eyes sparkling with humor and so much more. Desire? Want? Heat? She drew herself up—finally. "I am not attracted to you."

"Liar." A very slight dimple winked in his left cheek. "You really do blurt out the first thing in your head, don't you?"

Unfortunately. "I'm a little off, so give me a break." Geez. It wasn't every day a girl got shot at, kidnapped, and kissed in a way that only happened in romance novels.

"Livy, you're not afraid of me, and you know it. Instincts and all that." Smoother than glass, he reached around and secured her seatbelt around her.

She crossed her arms. Truth be told, she wasn't feeling afraid of him. He had saved her, and if he'd wanted her dead, he wouldn't have transported her a couple hours away in a very nice jet. Even so, being kidnapped had to involve some danger, right? "You and I are not on the same side." It was all she could think of to say.

He leaned back, his lips still curved. "Maybe not today, but if I've learned anything in my long life, it's that alliances shift quicker than an eye blinks."

His long life. Right. "What are you? Maybe thirty...two?"

He laughed. "You have to be getting hungry. I'll feed you the second we get to the ranch." Without waiting for an answer, he shut the door and crossed to jump into the driver's seat. The Jeep ignited with a low hum, and they sped out of the deserted tarmac.

She glanced around for some type of weapon, her mind spinning. Soon fields lined the way...and then cornfields? "Are you kidding me? Where are we?"

"Iowa." His hands rested easily on the steering wheel, in perfect control. "We have a safe house here."

"Who are 'we'?"

He shrugged. "Doesn't matter."

The hell it didn't. Night began to fall, turning the leaves of the fields ominous and so dark. Freaky, *monsters are inside here*, dark. She shivered.

He glanced her way. "What?"

"Cornfields. Creepy. Big monsters."

"Quite the imagination you have there. I obviously have been neglecting this place too much since the stalks are still up, even without corn. Why don't you write fiction instead of pseudo-facts?"

She chose to ignore the *pseudo* part. "I like facts and telling a story. Informing people instead of just entertaining them." Although someday she would like to pen a novel—maybe a journalistic thriller or something like that. "You can't tell me the snowy cornfields at night aren't a little freaky."

"Not a bit." He rolled his neck.

Figured. The guy didn't seem scared of much.

A farmhouse in the middle of an Iowa corn farm? "Who in the world are you?" she muttered, staring uneasily out the window.

"Somebody trying to save your life," he said just as quietly.

"I don't need you to save my life." Once she'd published the last article, the truth would be out there, so she'd be perfectly safe. "Why don't you just tell me the truth? How much do you know about the species with thirty chromosomal pairs?"

"Doesn't exist."

Right. The thought was unimaginable, but what if? Plants had fewer chromosomal pairs, while humans had twenty-three. What would a species with thirty pairs be like? Would they be immortal? Her mind had been calculating possibilities since Helen had reached out with the information, and she figured the species would be airborne. Made sense. "We both know the people who hired you have something more to protect than just drug patents."

"Really?" He turned his full focus on her. "How do we know that?"

Heat climbed into her face, and she tried to banish it. The guy looked deep into her, as if he knew. But no way could he know her odd ability—nobody knew about it. "Instinct."

"Right." He turned back to the quiet country road. "Now who isn't telling the truth?"

Her mouth dropped open, and she shut it quickly. He was just being sarcastic. No way could he know something about her she couldn't even explain. "I bet the species can fly." Made sense that they'd be a combination of God's creatures, and the ability to fly would be a step up from human abilities.

Chalton snorted. "Ridiculous."

She rounded on him. "How long do you plan to keep me in Iowa?" If she didn't escape, and she surely would, somebody would report her missing at some point.

He rubbed what looked like a granite-hard jaw. "I'm keeping you here until you give me the identity of your source and the location of all supporting documents. Then I just need you to sign a nondisclosure agreement, and I'll go on my way."

Something, and she wasn't sure what, sounded off in the statement. "What aren't you telling me?"

He sighed. "Nothing."

Lie. It was her gift, one she didn't understand. She could tell, almost always, when somebody was lying to her. And Chalton had been lying to her from the first second he'd opened his mouth. Such a sexy man shouldn't be a liar. "Are your orders to kill me?"

His head jerked back. "Of course not."

Truth. Interesting. "What if I don't sign the nondisclosure agreement?"

He growled low and didn't answer.

Yep. That's what she'd thought. "I guess it makes sense," she said thoughtfully.

"What?"

"That the extra-chromosomal species would kill to keep their secret. I mean, if humans knew about them, they'd be hunted and studied. We all want to be immortal." Yet she wasn't going to give up her story, because no doubt an advanced species would be able to cure human diseases. It was time they shared such knowledge. "Do you know any of them?" she asked.

He exhaled heavily and shook his head. "You are crazy, you know that?"

"I am not." For goodness sakes. She'd listened to Helen detail the science perfectly, she'd done her research, and then she'd read the proof in black and white. "I saw the studies and the results."

"Yet somehow the rest of the world hasn't?"

She nodded. "Yes. I saw copies of research from a couple of labs that no longer even exist. The labs themselves have been destroyed."

"Somebody is lying to you," he murmured. "This is about drugs and patents. Not a new species on earth."

Interesting. She couldn't detect a lie, but she wasn't getting a feeling of truth, either. So he might believe his story but have doubts, or he might be a phenomenal liar. Earlier she could tell, so now he might be shielding his lie better. Either way, intrigue kept her studying him. "You know what I think?"

"God, no."

She bit back a snarl. "I think you know the truth and that you work for this species that's immortal."

"I think you're nuts." He glanced her way. "Beautiful and spunky...but insane."

Warmth flushed through her followed by a welcomed temper. "If you take me back to the airport, or to a commercial airport, I won't turn you in to the FBI. I promise."

He grinned and swerved down a barely there driveway. "No."

Alone in the middle of nowhere with a sexy soldier hacker who might have kill orders on her? There had to be a way for her to get to safety. She studied the tall stalks flying by outside, snowy leaves glimmering in the moonlight. If she jumped out of the vehicle, she could surely hide in there, but what then?

"I wouldn't."

She jerked back toward him. "Excuse me?"

"The cornfields are dangerous at night. Creatures and all of that." Amusement deepened his voice.

"Jerk," she said, eying his fit form. "Why don't you have a gun?"

Tension emanated from him, filling the Jeep. "Don't like them and don't need them."

She narrowed her gaze. "Interesting. Was there a time you did use guns?"

"Yes, and that's all I'm saying about guns." He leaned forward to squint out of the front windshield at the moon. "We'll be at the farmhouse in about five minutes."

Good. Then she'd come up with a plan to get home. Hopefully Helen hadn't been scared off and would arrange to meet with the final proof again.

Chalton stilled.

Her heart rate rose out of instinct. "What?" she whispered.

He drew in air, his head not moving, his eyes roaming. "Shhh."

She pushed back in her seat, looking outside. Nothing out of the ordinary.

Chalton drew a phone from his back pocket, hit a button, and held it to his ear. "Dage? I think I might have a problem."

Dage? Who was Dage? And what problem? Olivia swallowed, her breath heated. What was out there?

Suddenly, lights rammed into focus behind them.

"Shit." Chalton muttered. "How far is backup?" he said to the mysterious Dage. Then, "Not good. Get the word out as soon as possible."

Olivia grabbed the dash and half-turned to see a lifted truck rapidly gaining on them. "Who is that?"

"Don't know." Chalton pressed the gas pedal, and the Jeep lurched forward.

A truck suddenly blocked the way ahead, and he slammed on the brakes. The vehicle skidded and then stopped. With a snap of his wrist, he flipped off the headlights.

Three men strode out of the cornfield to stand in front of the truck.

The vehicle behind the Jeep stopped, with the lights still glaring through the back window.

A lump settled in Olivia's stomach, and her hands shook. "Friends of yours?" She squinted through the front, trying to see better. The men looked...odd. Even in the soft moonlight, they looked incredibly tall and pale. Two had really dark hair with what appeared to be red tips, and the other man had red hair with dark tips. Some type of cult?

"Stay here." Chalton jumped from the Jeep and slammed the door. "You're trespassing, assholes."

The guy in the middle moved forward just a foot, spraying slush. "We don't want a problem with the Realm. Just give us the journalist, and we'll go."

"You take her and you have a definite problem with the Realm," Chalton said evenly, his stance widening.

What the heck was the Realm? Olivia moved to open the door, but Chalton shook his head, still facing the men. She stilled. Should she get out of the Jeep and help him? Or maybe she should let him deal with the men using the threat of the Realm, whatever that meant.

"Who's her source for the articles?" the tall guy asked.

"We've taken care of the source," Chalton responded. "Now leave. You can't afford another war right now, and you know it."

War? What war?

"We had her first, and we're taking her to headquarters," the guy said as his buddies fanned out.

Had her first? Did these guys work with the ones in the van?

"Thought you stopped hiring jobs out," Chalton said.

"It was daylight. No choice," the guy said. "Now hand her over."

So the guys in the van worked for these guys? Why couldn't they go out in daylight? Olivia quickly released her seatbelt.

"I've called for backup," Chalton said. "Leave now."

"No." With a battle cry that echoed over the cornfields, the lead guy charged Chalton.

CHAPTER SIX

Chalton pivoted and tossed the Kurjan over the Jeep. The soldier's elbows hit as he bounced to the other side. Holy hell. It was three to one, and that wasn't counting the force in the truck behind the Jeep.

How had the Kurjans tracked him to his safe house? He held his hands out to the men now angling toward each side of him. They'd worn dark clothing instead of uniforms, no doubt wanting to blend in as much as a Kurjan could. "Listen, guys. We want the story quashed as badly as you do, and I'll make sure it happens. Time to leave." If they didn't listen to reason, he was screwed. Backup was at least an hour away.

"No." The guy to the left drew out a green gun.

A laser-shooting gun that could take down an immortal. "That's not necessary." Chalton shifted his feet so he could attack.

"Sure, it is." The soldier pointed it at Chalton's head. "Olivia Roberts? Get out of the vehicle."

The door opened behind Chalton, and he could hear Olivia dropping out of the Jeep. She maneuvered up by his side, her heels sinking into the snow with soft plops. "If you don't mind, I think I'll remain with Chalton."

The soldier brandishing the weapon straightened. "Chalton? Reese?"

Damn it. Chalton partially moved in front of Olivia. A bullet from the green gun could easily kill her. "Nope. Not me."

The soldier he'd thrown over the Jeep crossed around the other side, blood covering half of his face. "This changes everything. I say we kill him."

"We're at peace, dumbass," Chalton drawled, his mind skidding into attack mode. If they killed him, they'd take Olivia, and she wouldn't last minutes before they figured out she was enhanced. The Kurjans had no problem forcing enhanced human females to mate with them. They were male only, just like vampires. "So time to go."

The leader smiled, revealing sharp canines that glowed yellow in the night. "We're not at peace, not really. We're just all regrouping. So you dying won't have much of an effect."

"Yes. Let's kill him." The guy with the gun took aim.

Olivia shoved in front of him, her hands waving. "No, no, no. Okay. Let's stop this." Then she stopped moving. "What's wrong with your teeth?"

Chalton grabbed her arm and pushed her behind him again.

She peered around his side. "Are your eyes...purple?" Her voice rose on the last. "Oh my goodness. Can you fly?"

The Kurjan frowned. "No." Then he pulled the trigger.

The laser impacted Chalton in the right shoulder, quickly forming a bullet and lodging in his flesh. He stumbled back and Olivia braced him with both hands. Pain exploded throughout his chest. "Get in the Jeep and drive through the cornfield," he grunted, keeping her covered.

"No," she whispered back, sliding out from behind him. "Don't kill him, and I'll come with you."

The Kurjan chuckled. "How about I kill him and you come with me?"

Stalk leaves rustled next to him, and a large body stepped out from the darkness. "I don't think so, asshole." Green lasers fired quickly, impacting both soldiers in front of Chalton.

"Theo?" Chalton said, shaking his head. What was his younger brother doing there?

The Kurjan to his left moved. Chalton drew the knife from his boot, dropped and rolled, slicing both Achilles tendons. The Kurjan screamed, fangs dropping, and fell to the ground.

Chalton levered up and punched the soldier several times in the face, hard as possible, until the guy passed out.

Grunting, Chalton shoved to his feet and turned, surveying the area. "There are—"

More bullets pierced his back, and he fell forward, rolling and trying to stand back up. Theo calmly aimed over him, impacting another Kurjan in the face, firing until the guy went down. "Came from the truck behind you." Theo craned his neck. "Looks like he was alone."

The bullets firmed inside Chalton, and he tried to remain standing and keep control. But pain ripped through him, and he growled, his fangs dropping low.

Olivia's eyes widened and she screamed, backing away against the Jeep.

Tingles detonated behind Chalton's eyes, and he could feel them change from black to a sizzling gold.

Olivia gasped and pressed her hand to her chest.

He smiled, blood gurgling out of his mouth. "Guess you were right. We do exist." Then he pitched face first toward the freezing snow, darkness slamming through him.

* * * *

Fear tasted like copper in her mouth. Olivia leaned against the Jeep, her chest heaving, her brain misfiring. Fangs. Chalton had actual fangs, as had the pale-faced guy. Her knees shook, and she tried to lock them in place.

On the ground, Chalton breathed heavily, out cold.

Run. She had to run.

Theo sighed. He had Chalton's size and dark eyes, but his hair was a shaggy brown around his collar. "There's nowhere to go," Theo murmured, tucking his gun in the back of his waistband.

Not true. If she could make it to the truck behind the Jeep, she could steal it.

"Listen, Olivia." Theo strode forward and grasped Chalton beneath the armpits. "The guys on the ground are Kurjans, and they'll torture you in ways you can't even imagine if they capture you. More backup is surely on the way, and if you take their truck, they will get you. Come with me and you'll be safe." He ducked and tugged Chalton up and over his shoulder in a fireman's carry, grunting with the effort.

She swallowed. "Ku-Kurjans?" The fangs could only mean one thing.

"Yep. Enemy of most vampires." Theo turned to stride toward a slight opening in the snowy cornfield. "I can't carry my brother and force you to come with me, so it's your choice. Kurjans or vampires? Up to you."

Vampires. Freakin vampires. And brother? So this was the younger brother. "Chalton is a vampire, and he's your brother," she said slowly, her brain just not working right. Shock? Yep. That was it. She was totally in shock.

"Yes. We're vampires, we won't hurt you, and we can't make you one of us. Everything you think you know is just silly legend. Pretty much." He crossed into the field. "Come or not," he called back.

She glanced frantically around. The Kurjan Chalton had punched was beginning to stir. Was backup really coming? How could there be real vampires? Advanced species, sure. But legends were correct?

The guy on the ground groaned.

Her feet launched into motion before her brain could even make a decision, running after Theo. She had to get away from the Kurjans, and now, more than ever, she had to know more about the species. Vampires. The only way to follow the story and stay safe, for the time being, was to run after Chalton.

Leaves slapped her, but she caught up to Theo. "So he won't die from the bullets?"

"No. He's strong enough to push them out of his body within an hour, probably." Theo didn't turn around.

A relief she probably shouldn't be feeling washed through her.

Her heels sank into moist earth, and small rocks tried to trip her up, but she scrambled after Theo, her heart thundering. How could it be true? Vampires. Real vampires. She'd been kissed by one.

Theo's face was longer and a bit leaner...but no less handsome than Chalton's. He moved with predatory grace as well. Maybe it was a genetic thing.

The smell of dirt and plants filtered around her, and the wind whistled somewhere in the distance. Strong moonlight allowed her to see the path, and when Theo took a sharp turn, she followed, stopping with a gasp at seeing a dark helicopter waiting quietly.

Theo turned and grinned. "I was going to make a bunch of crop circles to mess with Chalton but didn't have time." He shifted his weight, slightly jostling his brother. "Would you please look through your purse and pockets for a tracker? The Kurjans found you somehow."

She blinked and rummaged through her purse. "There's no way they could've gotten a track—" Her fingers brushed a smooth metal disk the size of a small battery, and she drew it out. "Well, hell." One of the guys in the van must've shoved it in there. Smart bastards.

"Throw it," Theo said.

She nodded and chucked it over several bare stalks. Life had gotten way too weird.

Theo reached forward and opened the back of the helicopter. "Get in."

She inched across uneven ground. Was this a good idea? Probably not. But waiting for more of the pale monsters seemed like a worse idea. So she lumbered inside and scooted to the far end on the plush leather seat.

Theo hefted Chalton in, allowing his head to drop onto Olivia's lap.

She gasped and then settled back. Chalton had to weigh over two hundred pounds of solid muscle, and yet his brother had just carried him without losing breath. Vampires must be wicked strong.

The door banged shut, and within a minute, Theo was in the pilot's seat starting the engines.

Quiet. The interior remained quiet. She frowned. "I've toured many areas in different helicopters, and we've always had to use headsets to talk. Why, or rather how, is it so quiet in here?"

"Technology. We have our own," Theo responded, lifting back on what looked like a small steering wheel.

Exactly. That was why she had to expose the species...to gain that technology and save Ronni. "I bet your scientific knowledge is impressive," she muttered.

The copter rose smoothly into the air. "We like to think so."

"Um, where are we going?" she asked.

He didn't even bother to shrug.

Chalton stirred, and his eyelids flipped open. "Olivia." Said as a statement, not even a hint of a question.

"You're a vampire," she said, looking down at his angled face.

He lifted an eyebrow. "Humph." Wincing, he reached for the hem of his shirt and began to tug the material up.

"What are you doing?" she asked.

"Need room," he grunted.

Geez. She reached down and helped him, drawing the bloody material over his head.

He settled back down with a satisfied sigh. "Thanks."

Moonlight cascaded in from the front, and instruments glowed around, illuminating the space well enough for her to see several bullet holes in his torso. His ripped, predatory, hard as a rock chest. As she watched, a bullet spit out near his right rib cage to clatter to the ground. The hole slowly closed.

"Holy crap," she whispered.

He turned his head to the front. "Theo? We have a problem."

Theo glanced over his shoulder. "One beyond the Kurjans?"

"Yes. What the hell are you doing here?" Chalton remained in place, his head rather heavy on Olivia's thighs.

Theo turned the wheel a bit. "I was hired to find Olivia and put an end to the articles she's writing about a species that has extra chromosomal pairs. Figured the Realm would have you on it since you're the computer hacker, so I, ah, traced your movements and was planning to take the woman at your vacation home in the middle of corn."

So it was actually Chalton's place? Weird. A vampire growing corn. Olivia frowned. "Wait a minute. Add in Jared, and that's quite a coincidence, right?"

"No," Chalton said grimly, shoving up to sit next to her. "That can't be."

"What are you talking about?" Theo asked.

"Jared was also hired to get her," Chalton said.

Theo looked over his shoulder, his face hardening. "Well, hell. All three of us on the same case? You're right. No coincidence."

"Call Jared and have him meet us at Benny's," Chalton said. "Nobody can trace the place to us, and we'll have time to figure out who wants us all on the same case in the same place. What common enemy do we have?"

"Just Peter Libscombe's kids, Petey and Saul," Theo said.

Tension wound through the luxurious craft, heavy and dark.

Olivia shivered.

Theo reached forward and typed something with one hand into an odd machine in the dash. "Sent the message, and I let him know we're being set up."

"Who is Peter Libscombe?" Olivia asked.

"Enemy as long as we can remember. Peter killed our father; our uncle killed him and then died in battle recently. Peter had two sons, although I didn't think they'd want to continue to fight," Chalton muttered as another bullet pinged out of his sternum.

Theo shook his head. "Saul is in South America on a peace mission. He'd never try to harm anybody. But Petey..."

Chalton nodded. "Petey is a chip off his old man's crazy block. Was a missionary for hire during the war because he just liked killing. But I didn't think he'd try to take all of us on."

Theo rubbed the back of his neck. "I've had a watch on both of them, and Petey disappeared about five years ago. I thought he'd probably died in the war, but now I'm thinking he's been laying low and planning."

"Agreed," Chalton said. "He's two hundred years old and loves killing. Avenging his father would be fun for him and not honorable. Just fun."

Olivia shivered. "Are Petey and Saul vampires?"

"No. Shifters," Chalton said.

"Shifters?" she yelped. "Shifters exist? I mean, people who shift into animals? Like birds?"

Chalton leaned his head back, shutting his eyes. "Shifters exist and can become canine, feline, or multis, which turn into anything of same size. Except multis don't seem to exist any longer and have evolved into different species of bears."

Holy crap on a double cracker. "Can you guys cure organ failure?" She held her breath.

"Why?" Chalton opened his eyes and focused on her.

She shrugged. "Just asking."

"Is that your motivation for these crazy articles? Your friend, Ronni?" he asked quietly.

Her head jerked back. "How do you know about Ronni?"

"I know everything about you. It's my job," he said simply. "As much as I'd like to help you and your friend, we are unable to cure human diseases."

How was that even possible? "I don't believe you."

"It's true." He rubbed the now closed bullet wound. "We haven't been much interested in science until recently, when we had to begin researching and ultimately curing a virus that harms us. We haven't meddled with human issues."

Issues. "You must have some knowledge that we don't. Or at the very least, equipment we lack. Look at this helicopter. And your phone. And your bullets." How dumb did he think she was?

He nodded. "The schematics for any equipment the queen felt would help humans has already been leaked."

"The queen?" she asked.

"Yes. Our queen was a human geneticist before mating the king, a vampire. Now she's immortal." Chalton wiped blood off his flat stomach.

"He changed her into a vampire?" Olivia whispered, her heart dropping.

Chalton grinned. "No. You can't be changed into a vampire. You could mate a vampire, and thus your chromosomal pairs would increase to immortality, but you wouldn't become a vampire."

Theo snorted. "Can you imagine? Now that's crazy."

"Definitely. Most legends are weird, especially the *have to suck blood* ones. We only take blood in cases of sex or war," Chalton continued.

Sex? She cleared her throat. "But I saw you...in the sun."

"Yeah. False urban legend," Charlton said. "Although, the Kurjans can't go into the sun, so maybe the legend is kind of a cross between vampires and Kurjans." He cleared his throat. "Theo, you're full of shit. No way did you go to all this trouble, waiting for me in Iowa, on the off chance I'd been assigned to find Olivia, so tell me the truth."

Theo turned the craft to the left. "Don't get mad."

"You asshole," Chalton said without much heat.

Olivia glanced at him and lifted her eyebrows.

He rolled his eyes. "How? I have firewalls that I even invented."

Theo grinned over his shoulder. "They were really good, too."

Ah. Olivia bit back a smile. "He hacked your computers."

Chalton shook his head. "Yeah, but you don't realize what a big deal that is."

"How so?"

Theo snorted. "Chalton is the best of the best. And I hacked him." Pure brotherly pride echoed in his voice.

Chalton jabbed two fingers in a hole near his sternum and yanked out a bullet to throw at his brother's head. "I'm glad you've kept up your computer skills. Come work with the Realm."

Theo hunched forward. "Only if Jared does. We're all in or we should be all out."

"Aren't you loyal, considering since you haven't spoken to Jared in a century?" Chalton muttered.

"Eh." Theo lifted a large shoulder. "A century isn't that long, considering we live forever. We've all been busy. I figured we'd all end up working together again at some point. So we should all be in...or all out. Don't you think?"

Chalton frowned. "It's not that simple."

"Yes, it really is." Theo clicked some levers on the dash. "Let's fight about that once we figure out who's trying to draw the three of us out at once."

"Good plan," Chalton said, leaning his head back and reaching for Olivia.

She blinked as he wrapped his huge hand around hers. Warmth and an odd feeling of safety filtered through her. She didn't know him, she sure as heck didn't understand him, but somehow, that simple touch calmed her as nothing else could have.

Of course, that just gave her one more thing to worry about. How would a vampire react to blackmail? She, unfortunately, was probably going to find out.

CHAPTER SEVEN

After Theo had landed the helicopter on the roof, Chalton led a subdued Olivia down the stairwell to the penthouse suite of one of the legendary apartment buildings in New York. How many laws had he broken by letting her know that vampires, Kurjans, and shifters existed? Probably enough to get them both killed.

Treason had become an unfortunate byproduct of his current mission. "That's why I stick to the control room," he muttered.

"What?" she asked, stumbling into him.

"Nothing." He also didn't like the silence coming from his younger brother, who took up the rear. It was almost as if Chalton could feel the guy thinking things through. Man, he'd missed his brother. Why hadn't he reached out before now? Fighting a war seemed like a lame excuse. He had to make things right.

They reached the vestibule, and Chalton punched in a code near the door.

"Where are we?" Olivia whispered as they entered the grand foyer of an opulent penthouse.

"Our great-uncle Benny's New York home," Chalton said, drawing her inside.

She glanced down at the sparkling fifties-style marble. "You have the code?"

"Sure." Chalton pressed a button near the door, and heavy drapes swung open across the living room to reveal the New York skyline. "He's in Europe this time of year, so his place is open for anybody needing to camp out." Chalton waited until Theo had entered and shut the door, leaning back against it, after assisting her out of her jacket.

"Talk," he ordered.

Theo flushed. "Well, none of this makes sense."

"Who hired you?" Chalton released Olivia's hand, and she moved past him and headed straight for the floor to ceiling windows and incredible snow-filled view. "Time to talk, Theo."

He nodded. "That's just it. I was hired by, well, mom."

Chalton stilled, the hair on the back of his neck rising. "Excuse me?"

Theo shrugged. "Mom is involved in a group investing heavily in different enterprises, and some of those are pharmaceutical facilities the Realm has used to research and manufacture the virus that formerly impacted vampire mates. Their stock has risen, mainly because of byproduct research, so mom's making a killing."

Chalton rocked back on his heels. "So she and her group hired you to track down Olivia? And do what? Kill her?"

Theo snorted. "Of course not. I'm supposed to bribe her to let the story go."

Chalton frowned, his mind spinning. "Was it mom's idea for you to go after Olivia?"

Theo frowned, his eyes sizzling. "No. Well, I don't think so. It seems like she mentioned one of her partners suggesting we tamp down on the articles talking about possible immortals."

Chalton nodded. "Okay. Go get mom, and get all the information you can. In fact, bring her here, just in case she's in danger from whomever is trying to get us all involved in this. Find out who told her to hire you." He reached for his phone and called Jared, having kept tabs of his brother's location and contact information through the years. "Where are you?" he asked when his brother snapped a greeting.

"On my way to have a little discussion with the group that hired me. Somebody is setting us up, and I'm starting with them."

Chalton nodded. "Good plan. Theo is getting mom and bringing her to Benny's. Apparently somebody got to her, too…and that's how he was hired."

"Fuck. I'll call you when I get answers." Jared clicked off.

Chalton shoved his phone in his pocket. "He gets more charming every year."

"Look who's talking." Theo opened the door. "I'll be back with mom. Bye, Olivia." He swept outside, and the door automatically locked behind him.

Olivia turned around, nicely framed by sparkling lights across the city. "Your family is very interesting." She glanced at the door behind him, at his bare chest, and then at a spot over his shoulder. "So."

"So." Amusement dashed through him as his body finished repairing itself. His injuries weren't bad enough for him to need somebody else's blood, but he'd truly love to bite her anyway. So far, he'd treated her with kid gloves, and now they had to come off. "I know it's been a long day, and you've had more than one shock to your system, so as soon as you give me the name of your source and the location for your research materials, you should catch some sleep while you can."

"No." Her eyes, tired as they looked, still spit sparks at him.

"No?" he asked, pushing away from the door.

She held her ground, her gaze turning very alert. "I will, however, make a deal with you."

"Is that so?" He reached her in several long strides, stopping just close enough to force her to tilt her head to meet his gaze. Intimidation was a necessary evil, and although he hated to frighten her, other enemies would do much worse. "Give me the terms of this deal."

She crossed her arms beneath her ample breasts. "Back away."

"No." His dick went hard as rock, and tension began to filter around them.

Pink climbed into her cheeks, and she licked her lips.

He bit back a groan. Why did she have to be so delectable? "What's the deal, Olivia?"

She cleared her throat, and a vein pulsed wildly in her delicate neck. "I've been thinking about the situation, and I guess I understand why you'd want to keep your existence private."

"Good."

She relaxed her arms and pushed back her hair. "I'll stop writing the articles so long as you fix my friend, Ronni."

Ah, what a sweetheart. "Who's your source?"

"My source stays protected." Her chin firmed into a stubborn, albeit very cute, rock.

"No." Regret tore through him, but he couldn't allow for emotion quite yet. "I have to know the identity of your source to figure out how they gleaned the information." While Olivia may not understand the issue, the breach in protocol merely ended with her. It had to have started somewhere else.

"Sorry. Source stays protected."

He rubbed his chin and studied her. "I want to be reasonable, but I have my orders, Livy. Give me the source, and I'll do my best to make sure he's protected throughout this."

Her nostrils flared. "You're lying."

He lifted his chin. Yeah. There was a good chance that her source was an immortal enemy that had wanted to draw out the Reese brothers, and as such, he would be beheaded for leaking such information. "How do you know?"

She shuffled her feet and broke eye contact. "Good instincts."

"Are you empathic?" he murmured.

She jerked. "No. I don't think so."

Interesting. "But you can tell a falsehood?" He'd never heard of an enhanced female being able to do so, but it could be an offshoot of empathic abilities, so it did make some sense.

"I just have good instincts."

Ah, the lies humans told themselves to avoid anything they couldn't rationalize with logic. He stepped right into her space.

"What are you doing?" she gasped, her chest rising.

He slid curly dark hair off her shoulder. "I'm facing a bit of a dilemma."

Her head lifted, although her gaze only reached his lips and stayed there. "How so?" Her voice lowered to a breathiness that licked along his cock.

"I need a shower to wipe off the blood and grime, so my choices are to bind you or have you join me." It was crazy, but he'd give his left arm for her to join him in the shower.

She half-coughed and half-laughed. "Are you hitting on me?"

His hand curled around her nape. "Yes."

Her gaze lifted to his, and her pupils widened. "That's insane," she whispered.

"I know." Hell, the woman was right. "But here's the deal. My brothers won't return for several hours, and then we'll have to move again. I want you, and you want me, so let's take the edge off so we can think." His mind hadn't been clear since he'd first sighted her two days ago, and he needed clarity. One good night, and he could get her out of his system. "What do you say?"

"I say you're crazy." She stepped back against the window. "If all I wanted was an orgasm to take the edge off, I sure as heck don't need you for that."

Humor bubbled up, and he full-on laughed. The woman was one of a kind. "Well then." His hands slowly went to unbuckle his belt, and he drew the heavy leather through the loopholes, quite enjoying the way her breath caught and her eyes widened. "Plan B it is, then."

* * * *

Every dark fantasy she'd had in her wild mind flashed through her brain. "Wh-what are you doing?" she asked, her lungs feeling way too full all of a sudden.

He grinned and continued releasing the belt.

Yeah, she was more tempted than she would like to jump his bones and just go for it. The guy was a vampire—a real, honest to goodness, vampire. Somebody with advanced genes could probably go all night, right? Probably all night and all of the next day.

She liked sex. Sure, it had been a long time since she'd tried it, and it had never been crazy fireworks time, but she'd liked being close to a man. Her last boyfriend, an accountant named Chuck, had taken a while to get going but had then been all right closer to the finish line.

Something told her Chalton didn't need any time to get going, and he'd probably be much better than all right.

Yet, she wasn't giving up Helen, her source, and so far, Chalton hadn't promised to save Ronni. Sleeping with him would be a colossal mistake, and she'd lose leverage. "What's up with the belt?" she asked again, eying the thick leather. A slow shiver wound through her body.

His grin widened. Shoot. He'd seen the shiver.

"Livy." His voice deepened to nearly guttural.

Desire unfurled in her abdomen. Then reality slammed her in the face. "Are you glamoring me?" she asked, anger rippling along her skin.

His eyebrows drew down. "Glamoring?"

"Yeah. What vampires do." She put her hands on her hips. "Making me want you."

He chuckled again. "Oh, you want me, and it's all you. There's no such thing as glamoring."

Truth. She opened her senses, and he was definitely telling the truth. "Oh." Then she focused on the belt, and her knees bunched to run around him.

Quick as a whip, he grasped her wrist. "That's a pretty blush you have there, gorgeous. What exactly are you imagining me doing with this belt?"

She stopped breathing, and her face heated to the point of pain. No way was she into all the "tie 'em up and spank 'em" rage going on right now. Yet there was something undeniably sexy about that leather in his strong, and no doubt capable, hands. "We, ah, are not on the same side here."

"We could be," he murmured. "If you keep publishing information about us, you're going to harm a lot of people. I know you don't want to hurt anybody."

No, she didn't. "All you have to do is save Ronni, and I won't publish another word. I promise."

He sighed. "We can't save human hearts, sweetheart. Hell, we can't even cure the common cold or cancer. We don't have the knowledge, either."

"There has to be something you can do."

He studied her, those dark eyes seeming to see everything. "There is one thing, but it's asking for a lot."

Her chin lifted. "What is it?"

"She's an enhanced female human, so somebody could mate her, and her chromosomal pairs would increase to near immortality, so her heart would repair itself."

"Enhanced?" Olivia asked.

"Yes. I searched her apartment when she was sleeping to see if your research was hidden there, and she definitely gives out vibrations. Strong ones. I'm guessing that's what drew you as friends, and I'm thinking she's probably psychic."

"I don't understand."

"Many human females are most likely distant cousins to the witch nation, and they have gifts beyond the norm like visions, empathic abilities, or many others, and they can mate an immortal."

"Mate?" Olivia's voice wavered on the end.

"Yes. It's forever, probably. So like I said, it's a lot to ask." He ran the leather through his hands. "Since this is my mission, I'd be on board. So if that's your final offer, it looks like it'd be me."

No! The reaction careened inside her and planted in her heart. "I assume mating means what it, well, means?"

"Yes. Sex and a good bite...and forever."

She blinked. "You said *probably* forever."

He nodded. "There was a virus that attacked vampire mates, hence all the research you found, but we cured it. The queen modified the virus, so technically the mating bond of immortals can be reversed."

"Technically?"

He shrugged. "The reversal has only worked on mates who've been widowed for centuries and not from currently living mates."

"Has anyone still living and mated tried?"

"No."

This was all so unbelievable. "Isn't there somebody else who could mate Ronni?" Not that Ronni would probably agree, anyway.

"My mission, my duty." He lifted a shoulder the size of a small mountain. "It's how it works."

Olivia kicked an imaginary pebble. "I want to save my friend, but I don't want to force you into a forever relationship with somebody you've never met." With somebody that wasn't Olivia. Geez. She had it bad for the guy.

"A lot of matings are arranged, so it's not unheard of in my culture." His gaze pierced hers and deep. "I do have one condition."

Tingles exploded throughout her abdomen. "Which is?" she croaked.

"One night with you."

Her entire body stopped moving, and her heart probably stilled for just a second. "You want to sleep with me as a condition?"

"There won't be any sleeping."

She slowly shook her head. "You're trying to blackmail me for sex?"

"It's extortion, not blackmail. And you tried to extort me first."

This was all just way too insane. "I can't sleep with you and then have you sleep with my best friend for life."

"Like I said, there won't be any sleeping. Look at it like different lifetimes...Ronni won't be here any longer if I mate her, and your friendship will be over."

Olivia blinked. "Why won't she be here?"

"My mate?" Both of his eyebrows rose. "She'll be somewhere safe at headquarters whether she likes it or not."

The possessive tone did very unnerving things throughout Olivia's body, the least of all creating a little jealousy. "I can't ask you to mate forever, even to save my friend. Besides, there has to be a cure out there. Your people must have incredible resources, and I'm sure they could find one to save a heart."

"Perhaps." Chalton rubbed his chin. "But I doubt it. The queen works brutal hours trying to cure diseases, and so far she hasn't succeeded with human ones." He dodged forward and tossed Olivia over his shoulder again.

"What are you doing?" she squawked, once again looking down at his fine ass.

"Done talking." Turning, he began to move through the living room.

Well that didn't sound good.

CHAPTER EIGHT

Chalton strode for the bedroom, a wiggly woman over his shoulder and fire in his heart. It would be his duty to mate Ronni, but every cell in his body protested vehemently.

He'd never believed in fate, and he sure as hell didn't believe in soul mates.

Yet having Olivia in the same space as him felt right. When she laughed, he could actually feel the humor, and when she seemed sad, every urge he owned pushed him to make it right.

Was she his?

If so, how could he mate her best friend? How could he mate anybody? Maybe he couldn't. There had to be something...more. In order to mate, there had to be that something that mated vampires couldn't even explain.

He didn't have the words, either...but he felt it for the woman now struggling to get off his shoulder. "Knock it off." He jostled her just enough to illustrate her precarious position.

She stilled.

He'd never drop her, but the threat was there, now wasn't it? She didn't know him well enough to understand he'd break every bone in his body before allowing her to get even a bruise. Good thing, too. The woman would certainly use that to her advantage.

He strode through the long entrance to the bedroom and dropped her onto the larger than life four-poster bed. She bounced and quickly scooted up to the headboard, her eyes wide.

And interested.

He sighed. "I also should tell you that the mating with Ronni might not work."

"Why not?"

"Because I'm interested in somebody else, and none of us really understand how or why we mate who we do. Some believe in fate."

Her hands curled into the thick bedspread. "Who are you interested in?" The tone came out accusatory and a little hurt.

He frowned. "You."

She blinked and her lips formed a slight O. "We just met."

"That doesn't seem to matter to vampires," he said wryly.

"I'm not easy," she spat out, seeming to be arguing with both of them.

He threw back his head and laughed. "Livy? I know everything about you, including past lovers. Believe me, your number is ridiculously small for somebody so gorgeous."

Her shoulders went back. "Oh yeah? What's your number?"

He lost his smile and fought the urge to shuffle his feet. "You don't want to know."

"Yeah, I do."

"Too bad. I've lived more than three hundred years, darlin', and I've had many careers...not once as a monk." Though every woman he'd ever met paled to nothing compared to the spitfire glaring at him.

His cell phone dinged, and he answered it. "Chalton."

"What the hell is going on?" Dage Kayrs growled clearly over the line.

Chalton kept Livy in his sight. "I'm not sure. This may be an attack on my family through Olivia. We're investigating. Also, the Kurjans are involved."

"Can't blame them," Dage ground out. "The first two articles more than hint at our world. Is the woman cooperating?"

"No." Chalton eyed her.

"Make her."

"Right."

Dage sighed. "Shall I talk to her?"

Temper, rare and hot, roared through Chalton. "You want to? Sure. Give me a second." He turned and typed in several commands on his phone, illuminating the massive flat-screen television across from the bed. Dage slowly took shape.

"King Dage Kayrs, please meet journalist Olivia Roberts," Chalton said dryly.

Olivia kept her arms crossed. "So you're the vampire king."

Dage's dark hair was ruffled, and his silver eyes pissed, but he looked every inch the badass soldier he'd always been, even in a dark shirt with pressed black pants. "Rumor has it. Why won't you give us your research and source's name?"

"Because I want to protect my source and blackmail you into saving my friend," Olivia said calmly while facing one of the most dangerous beings on the entire planet.

Chalton bit back a grin as Dage stopped moving and focused carefully. "I see."

Chalton edged a little closer to Olivia in case he needed to intervene. "You've read the reports and know about Ronni Alexander," she said.

"Yes. Heart disease. We can't fix that," Dage said evenly, his gaze not leaving Olivia's.

"I could mate her," Chalton responded.

"Oh, hell no," came an explosion from off camera before Dage's mate, Emma Kayrs, shoved her way into view. "You are mating for love and no other reason."

The queen had piled her dark hair atop her head and wore her customary white lab coat over T-shirt and jeans. Her belly had slightly protruded as her second trimester had begun.

"How are you feeling, Emma?" Chalton asked softly.

"Huge, but I'm not throwing up any longer," Emma said cheerfully, her curious gaze seeking out Olivia. "There will be no arranged mating."

Olivia scooted to the edge of the bed. "You're the queen? The scientist?"

"That's me." Emma leaned into Dage's side as if she belonged just there, which she did.

The king instantly softened somehow, putting an arm around his mate.

"Good. With all of your resources, you must be able to prevent heart failure," Olivia pressed, her concern riding the airwaves around her.

Emma frowned. "No, I'm sorry. I've been trying to mutate some of our research to cure cancer, but I haven't even been able to do that yet. The human body and diseases are so much stronger than current research." She sighed. "I'm very sorry."

Olivia sat back, her shoulders slumping. "She's telling the truth."

Emma's gaze sharpened. "Are you enhanced?"

"Apparently," Olivia muttered.

Emma glanced from Olivia to Chalton and then back again. "Well, isn't this interesting?"

Amusement glimmered in Dage's silver eyes. "Yes."

Emma pressed both hands to her hips and leaned toward the camera. "How are you even considering mating somebody else when, well, it's so obvious, Chalton."

One did not just tell the queen of the Realm to bugger off and mind her own business. "Nothing is obvious, Queen Kayrs," Chalton said gently.

She snorted. "You only call me that when you're irritated and trying to deflect."

Dage rolled his eyes. "Stop teasing Chalton. He doesn't have a sense of humor."

"Yes, he does," Olivia shot back. "He's very funny."

Emma's mouth dropped open, and Dage's cheek creased in a half-smile.

Emma turned to her mate. "Oh, this is fun."

Dage nodded and then sobered. "Seriously. How much danger are you in, and should I send backup? Talen has returned from Iceland, and he's pissy I sent you on a mission without him."

Chalton's chest warmed. He had two families—his brothers and the Realm. "Tell Talen I can handle my own mission."

"He knows that but feels left out." Dage spoke to Olivia. "Talen is my brother and our strategic planner, and he's the sensitive one around here."

Chalton chuckled. Talen was about as sensitive as a brick chimney. "Tell him to take up yoga and relax."

Dage laughed. "Talen and yoga? I'd pay a small fortune to see that." His smile slid away. "Seriously. How are you doing?"

Ah. There was the meddling, pain in the ass, too worried king that was more of a friend. "I'm fine, Dage. I haven't had to kill anybody, and the reunion with my brothers only involved a few bruises."

"Good." Dage studied him, probing deep. "It's time you made up with your brothers."

"I know." Chalton fought against the dull needle pricking his brain. The king was trying to read his mind. "Get the fuck out of my head."

Emma slapped Dage.

Dage shrugged. "Just checking. Good mental block, by the way."

"Thanks."

Olivia glanced from one to the other, looking a little dazed. "I think Chalton is fine—I mean, he was just trying to blackmail me into having sex with him."

Emma coughed, her eyes widening. "Chalton? Really?" Her gaze swung to him, and he could actually feel his face heating. "Was he successful?"

"I haven't decided," Olivia said, a smile in her voice.

Delight now filtered across Emma's face, no doubt having just found another best friend. "Olivia, we really must get together when this is all over."

"I'd like that," Olivia said.

Concern darkened Dage's eyes at the same rate it flew through Chalton's veins. "Not a good idea," Chalton muttered. Those two women together would wreak havoc.

"Agreed," Dage said thoughtfully.

Ah, hell. Now the king was going to matchmake.

Emma leaned forward to whisper, "You really should say yes. Even if it's just for one night. Sex with a vampire is truly out of this world."

Dage exhaled heavily. "Chalton? Call me with updates." With that, the screen went black.

Olivia cleared her throat.

"Who's your source? Extortion doesn't make sense any longer," Chalton said, wanting nothing more than to get back to his regular routine at this point.

She eyed him, emotion bright in her eyes. "They can't fix Ronni."

"No."

"Well then. I guess I'll take you up on your offer."

He rocked back. "My offer?" His voice came out hoarse, and his body roared into overdrive.

"Yeah. I mean, I just discovered that life is a whole lot different than I thought, and I do like a good adventure." She stood and turned to face him, her face flush with bravery and need. "I'll take the night…without sleep."

* * * *

What in the world was she doing? She'd just agreed to have sex with a vampire. In fact, forget the guy was a vampire. She'd just agreed to get naked and horizontal with the sexiest and probably the most dangerous man she'd ever met.

They did it horizontally, right?

"Why?" he asked, tossing the belt over his shoulder and moving toward her.

The scent of man and the warmth of male washed over her. "I want to." Sometimes life was as simple as that. Plus, her curiosity had gotten her far in life, and she just couldn't turn it off. "Do we really have to have an in-depth conversation about this?" Geez. Kiss her already.

"No. Just making sure this is what you want." He lifted her against his torso, turning to stride toward the bathroom.

"You're strong," she said breathlessly, grabbing his very bare chest for balance.

He grinned. "You're a lightweight, sweetheart."

She scoffed. "Not even close." Did she really want to get naked with such male perfection? Nobody had ever called her petite. Or small. Or fit. "Wait. I'm not—"

Then his mouth was on hers.

Hot and deep, he commandeered her lips, sending her senses spiraling. She moaned low in her throat and kissed him back, or rather followed his lead.

Still kissing her, he somehow reached into the shower and flipped on the water. Slowly, keeping her pressed against his muscled body, he allowed her to slide down him until her feet settled on the smooth tile.

She broke the kiss, her mind turning to mush, her breath panting out. A sense way too sharp to be desire sliced through her, making her want him with a craving that should give her pause. But it was too late to pause.

The look in his eyes was pure lust...and it was for her. He wanted her...all of her.

Drawing courage from that look, she reached for the hem of her dress and yanked it over her head.

The sound he made, low and guttural, vibrated through her body to land between her legs. "Beautiful," he murmured, reaching out to snap the front clasp of her bra.

Her breasts sprang free, and she shrugged out of the thin cotton.

He shoved off his pants.

Whoa. Okay. Vampires were built...really, really, really built. Hard and erect, he was ready to go.

Heat breathed through her, and she glanced around as steam filled the opulent bathroom. Chandelier on the ceiling, marble everywhere, top of the line towels. "Um—"

He drew her into the shower, and she groaned from the heated steam. Shower heads came at them from every direction, and she couldn't help a small chuckle from escaping.

He grinned and tugged her under the rain-shower head, which drenched her in decadent heat. Turning her around, he reached for a dispenser and filled his palms with shampoo before rubbing it through her hair.

She closed her eyes and tilted back her head, pure pleasure rushing through her. He had great hands. Then they moved lower, down her spine, to her butt. Her eyes flashed open.

Why hadn't she started doing lunges like she'd planned last month? "Um—" She turned, surprised a little when he let her.

"Um what?" he asked, shampooing his hair, his gaze never leaving hers. The suds ran down ripped muscles, corded everywhere, perfectly defined.

"This is a bad idea," she breathed, suddenly very aware of every dimple and curve she hadn't been able to banish. Edging to the side, she began to reach for the glass shower door, ready to flee.

"Oh, there's no running, little girl," he murmured, catching her arm and planting her against the tile. "If you don't want me or like me, then you're free to go. But if you're saying things in your head that you really shouldn't say about yourself, then we're going to have a problem." He stepped right into her, so male and sure. "And you really don't want that kind of a problem with me." One knuckle lifted her chin.

She swallowed. How could a threat sound so sexy? "I can think what I want."

He chuckled. "I thought so." Slowly, definitely deliberately, he set both hands around her waist and lifted her until they were eye to eye. "Put your legs around me."

She gulped and did what he'd said.

"Good." He leaned in, his breath brushing her lips. "If you were mine, I'd make you walk around naked all the time until you actually started to enjoy it and have the confidence such a beautiful woman should have."

Well. Sweet, and definitely sexy, but come on. Normally she was just fine with her confidence level, but being naked with perfection would rock anybody for a moment or two. "I don't need you to save me, Chalton. I'm fine."

He grinned against her mouth. "We all need saving once in a while."

Sweet. She liked him sweet. She leaned in and licked along his bottom lip, tasting salt and man.

His broad chest hitched.

Yeah. Power for the girl. She'd show him confidence. Her knees clasped his hips, and she dug both hands into his thick hair, taking his mouth. He allowed her to play, letting her go deep, before taking over and kissing her so hard her head was against the tile by the time he let her breathe.

Wow.

He flipped off the water and stepped from the shower, still carrying her like she weighed nothing. As if to prove his point, he flipped her around once before setting her on her feet.

She grabbed for his forearms to steady herself.

"Let's dry you off," he rumbled, reaching for a towel to thoroughly, very thoroughly, dry her head to toe, lingering in the good spots. Finally, she was on so much fire, she just grabbed the towel and dropped it. "Enough foreplay."

He fetched another towel, dried off faster than possible, and lunged. Within seconds, they'd cleared the bathroom and she found herself on her back on the bed with a heated vampire over her.

She reached up and smoothed back his thick hair. "You're beautiful," she whispered.

He grinned and kissed her, licking along her neck and down her jugular. She shivered. A vampire was kissing her above her freakin jugular. The erotic threat, the possibility of it, pulsed down her and between her legs.

He caressed along her skin, wandering across her collar bone.

She explored his shoulders, noting the strength, until he reached her breasts and tugged one nipple between his teeth.

Electric sparks flew straight from her breasts to her clit, and she arched against him.

"Nice," he whispered against her, flicking her nipple before wandering to nip and suck the other one.

She moved against him, her mind reeling. There was an edge to

Chalton, one just starting to emerge, that gave her pause and turned her on. He'd been so reserved so far...so in control.

Could she make him lose that control?

God, did she want to?

Right now so much need coursed through her she could barely grasp a thought, much less be logical. He continued moving down her body, peppering kisses along her abdomen before reaching her core.

She planted a hand on the top of his head. "No." Too intimate. Way too intimate. This was supposed to be a wild romp for fun.

He glanced up, between her legs, and allowed his fangs to drop low. Sharp and deadly looking, they stole her breath. He somehow smiled around them, and they retracted. "I'm going to play, and I'm going to be nice. Deny me again, and I'll use fangs."

She opened her mouth to protest, and he nipped her clit.

A mini-detonation rocked her, and she gasped, her head going back on the pillow. It felt too good.

Then he went at her. Slow and soft, fast and firm...he played her body like he'd designed it. Tension uncoiled in her abdomen, lifting her higher. So close. She was so close. "Chalton," she moaned.

He pressed two fingers inside her and sucked her clit into his mouth.

The room hazed, sheeting white. She detonated into a million pieces, flashing out, orgasming so violently her entire body clenched with the action. He prolonged the ecstasy until she fell back to the bed, limp, with a soft sigh.

Then he inched back up her, kissing everything on the way, levering right above her.

His face was all angles and firm lines, dark with desire. "Now we get serious."

CHAPTER NINE

Chalton fought every animalistic urge he owned to flip her onto her hands and knees and take her hard. The woman tasted like honey and heaven...and his. He'd felt her orgasm deeper than his own body, and now he wanted more. So much damn more.

She stared up at him, those pretty eyes wide, her expression bemused and a little wary.

Smart girl.

He shifted his hips between her legs, forcing them open wider. Her skin was softer than cotton candy and twice as sweet. Keeping her gaze, he began to push inside her. She was tight, even after her orgasm, so he took it slow, careful not to harm her.

She paused. "Condom?"

He grinned. "Don't work with vampires, and I can't get you pregnant unless we're mated." The instances where immortals had impregnated nonmates were too few to even consider statistically.

Her body enclosed him, taking him home. She lifted her knees, widening her thighs. Her body trembled around him in powerful aftershocks of her first orgasm of the evening. He wondered how many he could wring from her before she lost the sass and submitted.

He reached halfway and dropped down to kiss her, memorizing the shape of her lips and the taste of her mouth. He took her deep and had to shove hard to make it all the way inside her, planting himself to the hilt.

She gasped into his mouth, her body going rigid.

He lifted. "Take a moment and just relax." His heart beat like he'd run ten miles, but he had to give her time to adjust to him. He tuned in his senses, making sure the apartment was safe and no threat lingered near. Nothing felt out of the ordinary, so he focused back on Olivia.

She nodded, softening, her body releasing tension one muscle at a time that he could feel. "Man, you're huge," she said.

He barked out a laugh. How did she do that? He wasn't a guy who laughed much, and never out of the blue. Yet she brought out parts of him that had been long dead. "And you're soft. We make a perfect pair."

A small smile lifted her kissable lips. "You don't have to go with the sweet words. I'm not leaving."

He stilled and let some of his weight press her to the bed, reminding her of his strength. "I go with the truth, and with you, the truth is beyond sweet." Then he lowered his head to capture her gaze. "Knock yourself again in such a manner, and I'll fetch that belt."

Her mouth gaped, and spunk filled her eyes. "You're kidding."

"Nope." He'd never hit her with the belt, but he could think of a few ways to torture her a little with it. He hated the modern view of perfection being stick thin, and to think it had even messed with Olivia's mind a little just pissed him off. "Are we clear?" he asked evenly.

For once, she apparently decided not to push him. "Yes."

"Good." He settled his hips against hers. "Better now?" he asked, his biceps vibrating with the need to *move*.

She caressed down his flanks and over his ass, her nails slightly scraping. "Much better." She squeezed. "No mating, right?"

Sorrow, surprising in its intensity, slammed through him. Yet he forced a grin. "I promise I won't bite you." *Tonight* a small voice whispered in the back of his head. He ignored the voice and slid out of her only to push back inside.

It was like heaven and ecstasy and perfection all rolled into one devastating sensation. Her full breasts rubbed against his chest, and he could spend days just worshiping them. He leaned down to nibble on her earlobe, and her sex spasmed around his dick.

The woman was so responsive. What would she be like in full trust? As an enhanced female, she could mate an immortal who would have years to gain that trust. To see just how wild the intriguing woman could get.

"Does biting hurt?" she asked.

"Yes, but when you're caught up in the moment, it's bearable." His gums tingled with the need to let loose his fangs.

"Um, can you bite without mating?" she asked.

He nodded, trying to banish thoughts of biting her to the abyss. "Yes, we can bite without mating, but during sex it's a huge risk." He was way too attracted to her, and if he bit her during sex, there was a solid chance they'd end up mated. "I can bite you later, when I'm not inside you, to show you."

"I think I'd like that."

The woman was too curious, without a doubt. No wonder she'd become a journalist. "I could've bitten your thigh when I was playing, but I didn't want to scare you." So long as he wasn't thrusting inside her, he could bite her all she liked.

Her breath caught. "Oh." She tilted her hips to take more of him. He gave her more, adjusting his thrusts so each stroke, each delectable slide into her body, brushed him against her clit. Soon she began to tremble beneath him.

She'd thrown her head back, revealing the long line of her neck.

His fangs dropped, forcing him to concentrate on retracting them. The second they were safely out of the way, he increased the strength of his thrusts. Yeah, he'd have to go down on her again later and bite her thigh. Just the thought drew his balls up tight.

"What if I bite you?" she asked.

"Go ahead." The woman thought too much, and he was going to get her out of her head if it was the last thing he did. He reached between them, massaging a finger against her clit.

She moaned deep. "Wait. That's too much."

There it was. She didn't like being out of control any more than he did, but enough of that. "I think it's just enough." He waited until she shook her head, until she opened her mouth to argue, and then he pinched.

She gasped, arched, and her body climaxed around him, gripping strong enough to hurt. A small scream escaped her, and she shut her eyes.

To see her let loose like that was a gift he couldn't explain.

He pumped faster, keeping control, enjoying the bite of her nails against his flanks. Every time he shoved inside her, she went into another mini-spasm around him.

Fire lanced down his spine and gripped his balls. He let himself go, coming hard. Finally, he dropped his damp forehead to hers, more than a little surprised by how immense his release had been.

She murmured something beneath him, caressing small circles

against the small of his back. Offering comfort. He wanted to keep that sweetness forever with a fierceness that gave him pause.

Lifting up, he turned to the side and snuggled her into him. All woman, soft and fragrant, settled into him with a soft murmur. Without a doubt, he'd never felt like this.

She wiggled her butt to get closer.

Instant fire roared through him, making him hard all over again.

She sighed. "That was lovely."

Was? Oh, hell no. "Baby? We're just getting started," he whispered into her ear. They had all night, and he'd promised there would be no sleeping.

"Oh yeah?" she murmured sleepily. "What about that belt?"

Ah, the darlin' liked to issue a challenge, did she? "Want to be tied up?" he asked.

She chuckled, her body moving against his. "Not really. And that was wild, so how about we get some sleep and recover before round two?"

"Oh no." He wrapped an arm around her waist and dragged her lower half against his already rock-solid erection. "Forget sleep. Round two just started."

* * * *

Morning light filtered through the sheer drapes they hadn't bothered to cover the night before. Olivia flopped one leg out of the covers, her face buried in a pillow. She'd never be the same. Ever. When Chalton had said there'd be no sleeping, he'd actually meant it.

Sex with a vampire was over the top and out of this world.

Yet somehow, she figured it was more Chalton than his species. The guy was passionate, giving, and powerful. It was like he'd known her body better than she did.

With morning arriving, she should be swamped with vulnerability. But she was just too satiated, content, and relaxed to draw up any insecurities.

Besides giving her bliss all night, he'd peppered her with compliments that had the ring of truth. While she might wish she weighed a good twenty pounds less...he liked her just fine. More than fine.

His cheerful whistle echoed from the bathroom as he showered.

She blinked and shoved herself to sit, swaying just a little. Time to get back to reality. Glancing around, she spotted a phone near the bed. Who in the world still kept a landline? Uncle Benny must be quite the character. Chalton had said nobody could trace him to Benny, so the phone had to be safe to use.

In fact, she'd have to borrow it considering Chalton had thrown her phone out of the helicopter the night before so it couldn't be traced. She dialed, and Ronni picked up on the first ring. "Hello?"

"Ronni? How are you?" Olivia asked, worrying her bottom lip.

Ronni gasped. "Olly? Where are you? I mean, you said not to call the police if you went underground, but you didn't call, and I'm about two seconds away from reporting you as missing. What the—"

"I'm fine." Geez. She should've called. "I'm so sorry to worry you, but I had to chase a story, and you know how I get. More importantly, how are you?"

"I'm fine," Ronni wheezed, obviously not fine. "Are you still writing about the weird chromosomal mix-up story?"

"Yes, and I'm totally on to something." Okay. She just couldn't go into the existence of vampires over the phone. Or the whole mating aspect. She glanced at the partially open bathroom door. Could she really force Chalton to mate Ronni? Especially since she wanted nothing more than to get him back into bed and naked for the next century or so? There had to be another way. "I'm working on a cure for you," she whispered.

Ronni sighed. "Honey, there is no cure. I'm not a candidate for a new heart, and there's nothing that'll fix this one. You have to let it go. For me."

"I'd do anything for you." Even play chicken with the king of the vampires in an elaborate extortion scheme. There had to be a vampire out there who could mate Ronni that wasn't Chalton. Then they could get unmated with the mutated virus, probably. Yeah. Good plan. "I have so much to tell you, but we should meet in person."

"When?" Ronni coughed.

"Soon." The shower cut off. "Um, I have to go. I'll call you as soon as I can." She gingerly replaced the receiver and sat up in the bed, actually taking her first good look at her surroundings. "Whoa." Original oil paintings lined the walls, gorgeous and obviously one of a kind depictions of different cities at the turn of the century. Ornate furniture was angled around in a pleasing style...homemade and top of the line.

Uncle Benny had some cash.

Chalton stepped out of the bathroom wearing worn jeans and a dark T-shirt, towel rubbing his hair dry. "Benny only has jeans here, so it's casual day."

Her mouth watered. "Um, okay."

His phone buzzed, and he drew it from his pocket, sighing upon reading the face. He put it to his ear. "Hi, Dage." Within a second, he lost his smile, his face hardening to stone. "When? Great. Thanks." He clicked off and shoved the phone in his pocket. "Get dressed. We have to run."

She shoved from the bed and grasped her wrinkled dress. "Um—"

"Now, Olivia." He dodged into the closet to grab boots and yank them on before tossing her boots at her. "Go barefoot until we're in the garage. You won't be able to run in the heels, but bring them."

She yanked the dress over her head and stumbled toward the door. "What's going on?"

Chalton took her arm and began jogging through the apartment, grabbing her coat on the way. "Dage has been monitoring all chatter in New York, and he thinks there's a strike team on the way here."

Strike team? "The Kurjans?"

"No. He's smoothed things over with the Kurjans by telling them I mated you and you're no longer a danger to our world."

Mated her? Her heart thumped. "Then who?"

"Petey and Saul, who were sons of Peter. I figured someday they'd come after us, but not through you."

She shook her head, trying to keep up. "How did they find us?"

"I don't know." He drew a gun from the back of his waist and slowly opened the outside door. "Keep your head down. There's a back exit that isn't on the plans, but we have to reach the end of the hall."

She nodded and ran barefoot after him, wishing she'd taken time for a shower. They reached the end of the hallway, and Chalton shoved a pretty watercolor painting to the side to expose a keypad. He punched in a code, and the wall opened to reveal an elevator.

He tugged her inside, and the door smoothly shut.

An explosion rocked the building.

She stumbled and fell on one knee. He helped her up, rubbing her leg. "You okay?"

"Yes," she gulped. "What was that?"

"They probably breached the front of the penthouse." Chalton angled between her and the door. "This elevator goes to a secret parking area a floor below the parking garage, and it isn't on the blueprints, so we'll be okay. But we'll need to exit the garage, so they may see us."

She nodded, her heart thundering. "I understand."

"Good." He rubbed his forehead. "I just don't get how they found us."

"I don't know, but I was on the phone with Ronni just a few minutes ago. Do you think she's in danger?" Olivia clasped her hands together.

Chalton stilled. "You were what?"

His tone of voice, low and dark, shot adrenaline through her veins. "I, ah, called Ronni when you were in the shower."

"How? I took your phone."

"Um, yeah. I used the landline."

His eyes narrowed, and a flash of green shot through the black. "You. Did. What?"

"Um." Awareness, the kind that deer no doubt felt when faced with a hungry lion, rushed through her and cramped in her stomach. How did his eyes do that? "Your eyes just turned goldish."

"Vampires have secondary eye colors that come out when we're aroused...or furious."

Yep. Probably furious. No arousal there. Olivia tried to hold her ground. "I had to check on Ronni, and I figured the phone was safe since it's a landline and you said nobody can track you to Benny."

"I told you not to reach out."

"Yeah?" Fear morphed to necessary temper so she didn't start whimpering. "Well, I don't work for you."

He moved then so suddenly she didn't see it coming, pivoting and putting her against the wall. "They traced your call."

Well, hell. "It's not my fault they have some sort of tracker on Benny's phone." Geez. How in the world was she supposed to know that?

"They don't," Chalton ground out. "They must have one on Ronni."

Panic heated Olivia's lungs. She pushed Chalton, trying to get to the door. "How could they even know about Ronni?"

"They probably didn't. But I showed up in town, grabbed you, and I'm sure they investigated everything about you at that point. I didn't see this coming."

"So it's my fault. Then I have to protect her. We're going to her place."

"Right now, we have to get out of here safely." He shoved her behind him again, not so gently this time, as the elevator continued to descend. "Then we'll have a nice discussion about your lack of obedience."

Obedience? Did he fucking just say *obedience*? She punched him square in the kidney. "Don't even think about trying it, dipshit," she said, struggling not to yell.

He turned so suddenly she could only blink, grasping her wrists and yanking her toward him. His face, usually set in such calm lines, was a hard rock of pure fury. Danger seemed tame compared to him. His eyes glowed a luminous gold, and tension of the darker kind cascaded from him. "When the door opens, you will follow me and get on the bike without another fucking word. Got it?"

Instinct ruled, and she nodded numbly.

"Good." He turned back around, the muscles in his shoulders visibly vibrating and completely blocking her view of the door.

She swallowed several times, trying to calm her rioting nerves. Oh, they were so going to talk about his ass-backward attitude. When he wasn't so angry, of course. She was brave...not stupid.

Since the first realization about vampires, she might have had a rather romantic view of them as an immortal species. There was an edge present, an animalist, definitely predatory, aspect to him that she hadn't imagined. He'd hidden that part from her until this morning.

"Sex does change things," she mumbled, donning her coat.

His shoulders went back, but otherwise he didn't twitch.

She didn't want to poke the bear, but she had to say something. "Ronni is in danger if they're watching her. I have to do something."

"Ronni was perfectly safe with them watching her until you called her. Now she's in danger," he responded, his voice unrelenting.

Well, geez. Her fist closed with the need to punch him again, but caution won out this time. She'd probably pushed the vampire as far as she wanted at the moment.

The building rocked again. How many explosives were the Libscombe family using, anyway?

The elevator hitched and then kept descending.

Chalton growled low.

Olivia shivered and fought the urge to burrow into his back for reassurance. As much danger came from the pissed off vampire as from the explosives attacking Benny's nice penthouse. She hadn't given thought that one little phone call would result in an attack.

The door opened, and Chalton sprang out, gun at ready.

A garage-sized room held several motorcycles and what looked like a golf cart without wheels. Chalton made tracks toward a supped up Harley and swung one leg over the side.

She hurried after him, grabbed his arm, and jumped on the bike, trying to tuck her dress up for some modesty. Leaning down, she shoved both boots on her feet before tucking them on the foot step thingy. "I've never ridden a motorcycle."

He handed back a helmet. "Put this on, hold on to me, go limp, and let me guide you."

She nodded and shoved the helmet over her head.

The bike came alive with a loud roar.

She wrapped her arms around Chalton's waist and leaned in, allowing herself to find some comfort in his warmth. Sure, he was angry with her, but deep down, she knew he wouldn't let anybody hurt her.

He swung the bike in a large circle and aimed down a narrow tunnel. Bricks sped by, making Olivia dizzy.

Light became apparent, and they shot out of the tunnel into an alley. Bullets instantly impacted the side of the motorcycle.

Chalton swerved and opened the throttle on the icy roads.

Olivia screamed and shut her eyes, holding on with every ounce of strength she had.

CHAPTER TEN

Chalton positioned the bike the best he could, trying to keep his body between Olivia and any bullets. As far as he could tell, only one enemy soldier took post across the alley. A quick glance confirmed the guy's identity as one of Petey's soldiers. Chalton had kept a dossier on Petey's forces through the years, just in case. The rest were probably covering other exits, not even sure this was an exit.

The guy fired again, and pain rippled through Chalton's leg. Blood spurted.

He opened the throttle, and the bike jumped forward. Yanking to the right, he drove up on the sidewalk, putting vehicles between the bike and the shooter. A passerby screamed and jumped out of his way.

Olivia held on tight, her helmet against his shoulder, finally doing as he'd told her. He could not believe she'd made a phone call from the penthouse.

Smoke billowed out from the top floor, and several of the windows had been blown to bits. Glass and debris still rained down. Benny was going to kill him. Literally. Benny would literally try to cut off his head. It was nearly unimaginable how much money Chalton would have to offer to keep peace in the family.

He banished all thoughts of payoff and concentrated, using split-second reflexes to keep metal between them and bullets. Taking a sharp right, he then angled into another alley, turned left, and hugged several buildings before hitting the open and icy road.

The soldiers would come after them but wouldn't be able to catch the bike.

He took back roads as much as possible, and within an hour, his body began to relax. Unlike the penthouse phone, his cellphone was encrypted and couldn't be traced. Even though it buzzed incessantly in his pocket, he ignored it to keep driving away from danger.

Finally, they reached the warehouse district, and he pulled alongside a nondescript medium-sized metal building with logos for a bread company on the side. He tapped a keypad by a door, and it swung open, so he drove the bike inside.

The bike went silent.

Empty space surrounded them, while a small apartment was set in the far corner and enclosed by cinder blocks. Olivia used him for balance and pushed off the bike, stumbling back and taking off the helmet. Her stunning mahogany hair tumbled down over her shoulders. "You've been shot. Again."

He nodded and swung off the bike, wincing when his thigh protested. Reaching in the hole, he dragged out the bullet, biting his lip to keep from swearing. "I'm fine." Crossing his arms, he took a good look at his woman. Yeah. He was done pretending otherwise. "I am not happy with you."

She rolled her eyes. "Get over yourself. I had no clue about Ronni's phone being bugged."

"Hence my order to stay low and not contact anybody," he said evenly, holding on to his patience with both rapidly tiring hands.

"Perhaps you should've explained yourself better," she said sweetly, sarcasm in every line of her scrumptious body.

"Maybe I should've explained the consequences better," he murmured.

She stepped back. "You can't blame me for your uncle's penthouse being blown up."

"Yet I do." Could she not see she'd put her life in danger? If Dage hadn't been monitoring so closely, Olivia would've been caught in the crossfire. Chalton's phone buzzed again, and he yanked it to his face. "Damn it. What?"

"Benny's blew up. You okay?" Theo asked.

"Yes. We're at safe house three. You have mom?"

"No. Can't find her." Frustration darkened Theo's tone. "She went shopping, apparently, and didn't leave any more information with the house staff."

Chalton sighed. "Meet me here, and we'll figure out the best way to find our mother."

"Fair enough. You text Jared and have him meet us. It's time we figured out who's after us…other than the Kurjans."

"The Kurjans have been appeased, for the time being anyway. I saw one of Petey's men waiting to ambush me. We definitely have the right enemy in mind." Chalton said.

"It's about time. I'm tired of waiting for the bastard to make a move," Theo said grimly, hanging up.

Chalton nodded and quickly dialed Jared. "Jared, I need a favor. Will you pick up a friend of Olivia's? She's in danger." He quickly gave the coordinates. "Thanks. See you soon." He clicked off the phone and turned to study his woman. "Jared will bring Ronni here."

"What will you tell her?" Olivia asked.

He shrugged. "Let's figure that out when she gets here." Striding forward, he took Olivia's hand and led her out of the garage space and into the small apartment. She followed without protesting, which was a nice change. He released her and pointed toward the one bedroom and bath. "You mentioned a shower. There are clothes in the closet that should fit you."

She stilled. "Whose clothes?"

Did the woman sound jealous? He bit back a grin. "My mom's. This is a safe house for in case we need one…it's equipped for all of us." Somebody, probably Jared, had updated it throughout the years. "Go, Olivia." He needed a few minutes to regain control so he stopped wanting to throttle her.

She must've sensed his mood because she headed for the bedroom, stopping at the door to turn around. "Why haven't you and your brothers talked for so long?"

He turned, surprised at the question. "Our father died, and we were each in a bad place, so we turned on each other instead of to each other." It really was as simple as that. "But a hundred years for us is like a few weeks for humans. We just haven't had time to make up."

She leaned against the doorjamb, dark circles under her pretty eyes. "What bad places?"

He breathed out slowly. "Damn, you're a curious one. I had killed too many people, in war and out, and was facing a crisis of a sort. So I put up my weapons and turned to technology, which soon became computers as they were invented." Dage had saved his soul with the offer to work for the Realm as the computer expert and no longer as an assassin, without question.

"And Jared?"

"The love of his life, or rather, who he thought was the love of his life, mated somebody else. I never liked the witch." Chalton shrugged. "Theo had lost his best friend in a battle with an enemy shifter clan out of Africa, and he was blaming himself."

The timing had sucked all around. "We screwed up and should've helped each other instead of fought." Yeah, that was on him. He was the logical one and should've reached out before now. "It'll be okay, Olivia. I promise."

She nodded, pale and wan, and turned to disappear in the bedroom.

What was he going to do? If life were perfect, he'd court her for a decade and then make her his. As it sat, he'd promised to mate her dying best friend.

She reappeared in the doorway, buck ass nude. "Chalton? Want to join me?"

His cock sprang to action with an "oh, hell yes." Yet he shook his head. "I'm seriously pissed at you, Livy. Give me some time to cool down."

She snorted. "Don't be such a dork. Our time might be limited, considering we seem to be at war on several sides with pretty scary enemies. Let's take the moment."

His gaze swept down her curvy body and then back up, lingering on her breasts. Full and firm, they all but begged for his mouth. "You asked for it." Letting the beast in him take over, he strode toward the woman made just for him.

* * * *

Olivia swallowed and backed into the room, wondering once again at her own sanity. Adrenaline from the bombing and chase had been coursing through her system, and she'd felt brave. Chalton Reese, no matter his perfection, thought she was beautiful.

It was an intoxicating feeling, and it had gone right to her head. So when she'd taken off her clothes, she'd figured…why not?

As Chalton moved toward her with the grace of any predatory animal, her question was answered. He was pissed, he was dangerous, and he was unknown. Truly, she did not know him. Not really.

Now not only had she poked the beast, she'd pretty much punched him right in the nose with the dare.

"Um—" She took another step back.

"Too late." His expression matched his words. Stony and determined...and so damn male. He reached her and threaded his fingers through her hair, tangled, and pulled her right up on her toes.

She gasped, opening her mouth, and he took full advantage. Driving his tongue in, dueling with hers, bending her back to be kissed hard. His other hand clamped on her hip and yanked her into pure male muscle.

The whimper up her throat would've embarrassed her if her mind wasn't spinning. She was naked, and he was fully clothed, swamping her with a heated vulnerability she shouldn't have liked. Yet she kissed him back, unable to move an inch, desire rushing through her stronger than hundred-year-old cognac.

He broke the kiss and lifted her easily, all but tossing her on the bed. She bounced once, and then he was on his knees on the floor, his mouth on her core, her legs over his shoulders.

She tried to sit up, to protest, but one hand flattened over her abdomen.

He glanced up, his eyes a burning gold. "Stay in place."

The spit on her tongue dried up, and she froze.

"Down," he ordered, no give on his chiseled face.

She blinked once and then lay back down, her heart beating so fast her ribs ached.

He licked her, humming with pleasure, and nipped her clit.

Sparks flew through her so hot and fast she could only gasp. Then he went at her, licking, nipping, and biting...in perfect rhythm, until she was a mass of aching nerves ready to beg.

She glanced desperately around the small bedroom. Black and white photographs of airplanes through the years covered the walls, and a heavy oriental rug sprawled across the concrete floor. He nipped her again, and she closed her eyes against the heated bliss.

"Chalton," she moaned.

He released her and turned to rub his nose against her thigh. She gyrated against him, needing much more, so close to the edge a strong breeze would carry her over.

Pain lanced through her thigh.

She partially sat up, and the hand on her abdomen pushed her back down. He'd bitten her. His tongue made quick use of closing the wound, and then landed square on her clit.

She whispered his name, fireworks flashing behind her closed eyelids. The orgasm rolled through her, pounding, stronger than any lightning strike. He prolonged the waves, using his mouth and his fingers, until she flopped back down with a low moan.

Then he stood.

She tried to form words, but nothing would come.

He ripped his shirt over his head, revealing all of that smooth, strong muscle. Then his pants hit the floor.

No way could she join him this time, but he definitely deserved an orgasm. So she widened her thighs.

Slowly, he shook his head, raw need in his dark eyes.

She frowned.

He grasped her hands and tugged her to stand. Her legs wobbled. Then he turned her around and lowered her to her hands and knees on the bed, facing the headboard. Strong hands grabbed her hips, and he thrust inside with one controlled shove.

She sucked in air and dug her nails into the dark bedspread. Holy crap he was huge. A feeling, an uncoiling, started deep inside her. How was that possible?

He flattened his hand between her shoulder blades and pushed down until her head hit the covers. She turned to the side to breathe, a powerful predator behind her.

Open and vulnerable, she could only feel.

So much heat and undeniable power. Yet she had to ask. "Is this because you're mad?"

He stopped moving, buried balls deep inside her. "Does this feel mad?" he asked.

No, it felt fucking amazing. He was so deep she wasn't sure where he ended and she began. "No, but I wanted to make sure." Her voice was muffled in the covers.

He slid out and powered back inside her. "This is for fun and because it feels good. This"—he smacked her ass and hard—"is because I was pissed."

"Ow," she howled. Then, because he'd surprised her, she laughed out loud.

He paused again. "You're laughing?" Amusement darkened his tone.

She shivered from the tenor and laughed again. "I can't help it. You surprised me, and that's how I react." And yet, she was having fun.

Without question.

"Interesting." He peppered several smacks to her rear end, and she stopped laughing altogether. "Better."

Oh, he did not. Worst of all, since he was firmly implanted inside her, every smack had ricocheted sparks throughout her body. Somehow he ignited her desire again, this time into a hunger that actually hurt.

"I might have to harm you," she gasped into the bedclothes.

A slap to the center of her ass had her arching and riding the fine edge between pain and pleasure.

"So that's how to quiet you," he murmured, rubbing her heated flesh.

Her mind caught his meaning several seconds after her body had spasmed. "Hey—"

SMACK.

She arched again, taking more of him in.

He chuckled a low rumble, grasped her hips, and began pounding with a harsh rhythm that took her completely out of reality. The slap of flesh against flesh filled the room along with their ragged breathing.

He pulled her back to meet his thrusts, controlling her, taking her places she hadn't known existed.

She broke with a low cry, the orgasm taking her over, filling her with so much pleasure she could barely breathe.

He shuddered and fell over her, his lips brushing her ear.

Slowly, he pulled out, and she felt a sense of loss way out of proportion for the moment. He turned her over, pushed her up on the bed, and sprawled over her, his elbows taking his weight.

"You okay?" he asked, pushing damp hair away from her face.

She nodded, too much emotion swamping her to allow speech. If she talked, she'd say something really stupid about love and destiny. She'd lost her mind. A couple of amazing orgasms and she'd gone crazy.

He placed a gentle kiss against her lips. "You feel it, right?"

She nodded again, wanting nothing more than to stay right there, in his arms, forever. How nuts was that?

"Me too." He kissed the corners of her mouth, her nose, her cheeks, even her eyelids.

A rumble sounded from outside.

He drew her up and off the bed, patted her still smarting ass, and pushed her toward the bathroom. "That's one of my brothers. Take a quick shower. We'll figure everything out later."

She nodded and hitched toward the bathroom, small aches and pains springing to life. He felt like hers, but what about Ronni? What would she give up to save her best friend's life? How could she ask Chalton to give up his freedom for eternity?

CHAPTER ELEVEN

Chalton dragged on the borrowed jeans, leaving them unbuttoned while padding barefoot into the vast garage space. Theo arrived on an impressive looking Ducati seconds before Jared roared in on a Harley with a pale brunette holding on for dear life behind him.

The second he killed the engine, she pushed off the bike. "You are such a complete dickhead of an asshole," she muttered.

"I told you to hold on," Jared said calmly, swinging off the bike and turning on Chalton. "Miss Temper here didn't want to come, so I had to convince her."

Ronni rounded on him, both hands on her too slender hips. "This is kidnapping, and you better believe I'm going to press charges on your ass."

Theo grinned. "What in the world did I miss?"

"You're an accessory, asshole," Ronni snarled, her Columbian accent sharpening the words.

For a feisty brunette, she really was cute. Long hair, deep brown eyes, curvy figure. Not Chalton's type, but if he remembered right, Jared had a thing for women from romantic countries. Spunky women.

Though by the thunderclouds gathering in his deep eyes, he didn't have a thing for this one.

Chalton cleared his throat. "Ronni? Olivia is through that door taking a quick shower. I'm sure she'd like to see for herself that you're all right."

Ronni gave him one of the most scalding looks he'd ever received before lifting her head high and stomping through the room and out of sight. The apartment door slammed behind her hard enough to rattle the outside door.

"She's ill," Jared said, eyebrows raised.

"Yes. Heart problems," Chalton said.

"I could smell it on her, but she sure as shit doesn't let it slow her down," Jared muttered, rubbing his jaw. "The girl knows how to hit." Now he sounded impressed.

"Well, at least she's a fighter. I've offered to mate her to save her life," Chalton said, his gut aching.

Jared rocked back on size sixteen boots. "You smell of another female, brother. Planning a harem?"

"No." He frowned. "Things have gotten a little out of hand."

"Fuck. I leave you alone for one little century, and now you've got two women to mate. You know you can only mate one, right?" Jared drawled.

"Asshole," Chalton said without heat. "Did you find the people who hired you to track down Olivia?"

Jared growled. "No. They seem to have disappeared, but don't worry, I will find the bastards." He turned toward Theo, who was watching the exchange with barely contained amusement. "Where the hell is our mother?"

Theo sobered. "No clue. She doesn't check in with me any more than you, and she gets irritated if any of us get too overbearing."

"I called her, but she hasn't responded," Chalton muttered.

"Me too," Jared said.

Theo glanced at his phone. "She hasn't called me back, either." Then his phone buzzed, and he grinned. "There she is. She called me first." Triumph lightened his hard face as he answered the phone. "Hi, Mom." His smile disappeared, and he cut a look at his brothers. "Who the fuck is this?"

Chalton stopped breathing, his body settling into battle mode. "Record it," he mouthed, charging closer to his brother as Jared did the same.

Theo nodded and hit a button on his phone. "Let me see her." He glanced down at the phone, holding it out so they could all see their mother tied up, furious, in a chair.

Petey Libscombe came into view. The years hadn't been good to him. His hair had thinned, very rare for a shifter. "You had to know I'd be coming."

Chalton shrugged. "We figured you'd be out trying human balding cures."

Theo snorted.

Petey growled low and stepped behind their mother. "As you can see, I've taken good care of your mommy. She's at her little hidey-hole in the city, perfectly unharmed. Be here in an hour or I cut off her fucking head." The picture went dark.

Theo turned and ran toward the apartment, stopping in the small living room and connecting the phone to the huge plasma television to bring up the recording for a wider view. Their mom slowly took form on the massive screen. "Where is her hidey-hole in the city?"

Chalton shook his head.

"No clue," Jared said, his voice sounding like death on a promise.

Chalton growled. "I don't understand. How can she have a place in the city we don't know about? What does she do there?" He spoke with her several times a week, and not once had she mentioned a getaway place.

Theo ran through the video frame by frame. "Nothing here shows us where she is." He froze the screen. Their mom sat, tied and gagged, on a purple office chair. A bookshelf lined the wall behind her, stacked high with tons and tons of books. Her brownish hair curled around her shoulders, and her dark eyes shot furious sparks.

Rage threatened to cut off Chalton's ability to think, so he took several deep breaths to regain control. It was unthinkable, even in times of war, to go after females, and especially somebody's *mother*.

"I'm going to cut off his nuts and feed them to his brother," Jared said, his fingers curled into fists.

"His brother is in Morocco right now and probably not a part of this," Theo muttered.

"Don't care," Jared responded.

Olivia walked out of the bedroom wearing a cute black yoga outfit that showed off her curves to perfection, leading a bewildered looking Ronni. "I know it sounds crazy, but it's all true. There are actually people who turn into animals, although I haven't seen that happen yet. For now, it's just vampires and the weird white-faced dudes." She glanced up at the screen and stopped cold, her face going white. "What did you do?" she whispered.

Chalton frowned. "We didn't do that."

"I don't understand." She walked closer to the screen. "Why would anybody hurt Helen? Where is she? What's going on?"

Shock clipped through Chalton. He grasped Olivia's arm and flipped her around. "How do you know my mother's name?"

Olivia's mouth dropped open and then closed with a snap. "Your *mother?*"

"Yes." Oh, he so did not like where this was going. "Again, how do you know her?"

Olivia pressed a hand to her stomach. "She's my source for the story. I mean, everything I know about immortal species came from her."

* * * *

Olivia caught sight of Ronni's too pale face and drew her forward to sit on the lone leather sofa in the barren room. Telling her about immortals had been more difficult than she'd thought. Maybe the innocuous living space would help calm her friend. The television took up one wall, the bedroom entry the other, pictures of airplanes the third, and behind them was a utilitarian kitchen.

Ronni sat, her hands trembling. "Those are not vampires. Vampires don't exist."

"Chalton?" Olivia called.

He eyed them, let his fangs drop, and then growled.

Ronni gasped.

Chalton rolled his eyes and let his fangs retract. "We have bigger issues right now to deal with. Why the hell did my mother give you proprietary information?"

Olivia shrugged, her mind spinning. "I don't know. She called me up out of the blue, said she had read my articles about the North Platt labs using animals for testing, and that she had a great story for me. When we met, she gave me the first few documents about missing information."

Chalton rocked back on his heels, thoughts scattering across his face. Dark-looking thoughts. He glared at Jared. "Any ideas?"

"None I like having," Jared retorted, crossing arms that looked firmer than steel and twice as strong. "Theo?"

"Dunno." Theo shrugged.

"Considering our mother basically committed treason against, well, everybody...maybe we should figure this out," Chalton snapped.

Jared shook his head. "If the Realm finds out about this, they'll cut off her head."

"No, they won't," Chalton returned.

"Oh yeah? Why the hell not?" Jared hissed.

Chalton rose to his full height. "Because Dage Kayrs is my friend, and you don't cut off the head of your friend's mother." By the time he finished the sentence, he was yelling.

"Bullshit," Jared yelled back, stepping within punching distance.

"You have always had a hard-on for the Realm, and it's time you fucking made peace," Chalton bellowed.

Jared grabbed him by the lapels and leaned in. "I don't give a shit about the Realm and never have. So long as they stay out of my way, I'm fine."

"They've never been in your way," Chalton yelled into his brother's face, arms shooting up to break the hold. Every inch of his body wanted a brawl, and he braced to take the punch that was no doubt coming.

"Stop it right now," Olivia yelled, her voice much higher than theirs.

They both stopped, their heads swinging to look at her.

She stood and planted her hands on her hips. "Far as I can tell, the last time you got into it, you didn't speak for a hundred fucking years. So how about this time you work together, get your mom back, and act like brothers?" Her voice rose high enough at the last that Chalton winced.

"Your woman is loud," Jared said, backing up to sit next to Ronni on the sofa.

"I am not his woman," Olivia screamed, her face turning red.

Ronni cleared her throat. "It kind of seems like you are." When Olivia swung an irritated look back at her, she shrugged. "Well, it does."

"I can't be," Olivia whispered.

Ronni smiled at her and turned that smile on Chalton. "Hey, so I appreciate the offer of mating and all of that, even though I think you're all certifiable. But I am so not mating the guy my best friend loves. Sorry."

"I don't love him," Olivia snapped.

"Yes, you do," Chalton bit out. It was one thing to play hard to get or to take time to figure out feelings, but no way was she going to lie out loud to him. "It happens fast with vampires, so deal with it."

"What about Ronni?" she asked, pain slicing through her. "She'll die."

Ronni reached up and tugged Olivia down to sit. "We all die." Then she glanced around the room. "Okay, maybe not. But most of us do." She frowned and glanced sideways at Jared. "Is this possibly a trick? The whole vampire thing?"

He lifted an eyebrow and let his fangs slide out. "Feel."

She gingerly reached out and ran a finger down the wicked canine. "Feels real."

It retracted.

She leaned away from him. "You're sure you won't suck all my blood out and turn me into the undead?"

Jared rolled his eyes. "Jesus."

Chalton glanced at their helpless mother on the screen. "We have got to find her place in the city."

Olivia cleared her throat. "Um. I know where that is. It's actually my private office in the city. I gave Helen a key because she wanted a quiet place to go, and we arranged for her to leave me information there for the story. It's where my laptop and all my notes are hidden."

More tension roared through the room, and Olivia fought the very real urge to run like hell. "I can, uh, draw a diagram of the building and outlying area, if you'd like."

Chalton nodded, his eyes black orbs of pure fury. "Is there any chance our mother told you why she decided to betray the immortal world?"

Olivia cleared her throat, trying to remain calm. "Um, no. She didn't mention she was immortal."

"No reason at all for giving up the information?" Jared asked, tension cutting lines in the side of his mouth.

"She just said that she had information that had to get out there, and that the researchers behind the studies had all disappeared. She felt that the medical advancements being hidden could be an impressive help with human illnesses." Olivia smoothed her hands down the thick yoga pants.

"So she knew about Ronni," Jared drawled. "She used your motivation against you."

"I think she really wanted to help," Olivia countered.

"Did she mention us?" Theo asked, rubbing his jaw.

Olivia shook her head. "Your mom looks about forty years old, so if she'd mentioned three grown sons, it would've been a red flag, don't you think?"

"Good point," Chalton said grimly. "All right. I'll contact the Realm and get satellite imaging going for the building, while you start diagraming."

Jared pushed to his feet. "You know this is a trap, right?"

"Right." Chalton nodded. "Definite trap."

Olivia stood and then faltered. "If it's a trap, how can you go in?"

"It's our mom," Chalton said. "No choice. So let's get as prepared as possible."

Well, that was just fantastic. What could go wrong?

CHAPTER TWELVE

Olivia ignored her extremely pissed off lover and kept flush against the building, adrenaline shooting through her veins faster than a motorcycle at full throttle. A gun lay heavy at her back beneath a buttery-soft leather jacket, and a knife scratched against her calf inside a badass leather boot.

Chalton's mom knew how to dress apparently.

Ronni, similarly armed, nudged her. "I'm thinking we're idiots for coming," she whispered.

Olivia swallowed down bile. "I know." Yet she was a journalist, and stories sometimes became dangerous. She started this one, and she'd by damn finish it.

Chalton cut her a look from across the doorway of the older brick building. He'd ordered her to stay at the warehouse, but both she and Ronni had insisted on coming. When he'd decided just to tie them up, Theo had intervened, saying that they had a right to finish this out, too.

Jared had agreed with tying them up, his gaze remaining pretty hot on Ronni.

But the satellite pictures with heat signatures illustrated that Petey was long gone from the office. The pictures showed a lot of people in the vicinity but no guns. Well, no visible guns. They could be hidden, and Petey might be nearby ready to strike.

Chalton was a different man in battle. Hard, cold, and meticulous...completely banishing the lover who'd rocked her world last night. For the first time, she could see the assassin he used to be.

No doubt he'd kill to protect his mother, but Olivia said a quick prayer that he wouldn't have to do so. What would that do to him?

He gave some weird hand signal. Jared nodded and yanked open the quiet green door, while Theo tensed behind Ronni.

Chalton went in first, Jared second, then Olivia hustled after him, trusting Theo to protect Ronni. Even now, her breathing was labored behind Olivia.

There had to be some way to save her.

Jared lifted some cool-looking scope down the hallway and gave a quick nod. Several doorways lined the way, all to small offices, all seemingly quiet since it was Sunday.

They reached the third office on the left, and Jared pointed the scope at the door. Olivia stood up on her tiptoes to see the readout, which showed the heat signature of one person tied up on a chair. A smaller person. It had to be Helen.

Jared meticulously ran the scope around to see the entire office. No heat signatures...no other people.

Olivia breathed a sigh of relief. Okay. So the trap wasn't inside.

"They'll be waiting when we leave," Chalton whispered.

Jared nodded. "I have men closing in on the area. If there's a threat, they'll find it."

"The shifters are still an hour out, but they'll be here as soon as possible," Chalton said, having called for more backup the second they'd formed a plan.

"If Petey is around here, waiting to take a shot, he's mine," Jared said.

Chalton shook his head. "Whoever has the shot can take it."

"It won't be a shot, and you've come too far to return to darkness," Jared said.

Chalton studied him but didn't answer. "Ready for go?"

Jared's face hardened even more and he nodded.

"Ready," Theo said, his voice strong and determined.

Olivia tensed, ready to jump inside and do something. Anything. Okay. Duck and cover.

Chalton kicked the door in and went in low, while Jared went in high. Theo covered Olivia and Ronni in the hall.

"Clear," Chalton called out.

Olivia ran inside just as he was gingerly removing the gag from Helen's mouth.

"Get out," Helen screamed, struggling furiously with her bindings, tears streaming down her face. "Now. Go."

The door slammed shut behind Theo, and he turned to pound on the heavy oak. An explosion rippled through the hallway outside, and ceiling tiles rained down in the office.

Chalton drew a knife from his boot to cut his mother's bindings.

Jared rushed for the window.

"Stop. It's wired," Helen hissed.

Jared slowed down and peered up and then surveyed the windowsill. "Yep. Wired from the outside."

Ronni hitched to his side and bent down to survey the outside sill. "Mercury lever. If we lift the window or even try to break the glass, the vibrations will make it blow."

Jared glanced down at her.

Ronni shrugged. "I haven't always been dying, you know."

"You work with a bomb squad?" Jared asked.

Ronni scoffed. "No. I'm a police shrink. But the job gives me access to tons of different classes, and bombs are interesting."

"Can you diffuse one?" Jared asked.

"No." Ronni blanched. "Sorry."

Helen stood and was instantly enfolded by Chalton. She shoved him. "What are you three doing here? It's a trap. You had to know it's a trap."

"Of course it's a trap," Chalton said, gingerly touching a bruise at her hairline. "Are you all right?"

She rolled her eyes. "Of course I'm fine. I'm just bait, you know." Irritation wrinkled her forehead. Then she caught sight of Olivia. "Oh no. What in the world are you doing here?" Rushing forward, she gathered Olivia in a lilac-scented hug.

"I came to help save you." Olivia returned the hug and then levered back to study the shorter woman. Since Olivia's parents had died when she'd been young, she'd enjoyed the maternal comfort provided by Helen. "So. There's quite a bit you didn't tell me."

Helen smiled, her dark eyes identical to Chalton's. "True."

"How could you lie to me and get away with it?" Olivia asked. "I can usually tell."

Helen smiled. "I've been immortal for centuries, dear. Masking a lie isn't as difficult as you'd think."

"Why, mom?" Jared asked, gently leading Ronni away from the wired window. "Why in the world would you leak proprietary information and put a bounty on your head?"

Helen shrugged. "I figured the king would send Chalton to

investigate. I hired Theo, and I had friends of mine hire you to all track down Olivia."

"Why?" Chalton asked, his eyebrows drawing down.

"You boys haven't talked in over a hundred years."

Helen put both hands on her hips. "I thought that having a common goal would get you in the same place, and look! It worked."

"Is that all?" Theo asked, a smile barely lifting his lips.

"Um." Helen shuffled stunning black Manolo's. "Well, I did notice that Olivia was enhanced. As is Ronni, by the way."

Chalton groaned. "This is some elaborate matchmaking scheme?"

"Well, it was, but I admit it got out of hand. I didn't expect Petey to make a move." Helen swallowed. "It's my fault. Obviously he was watching me, and when I arranged for you all to be here at the same time, he finally made a move. I'm so sorry."

That did explain the timing. Chalton strode toward the crumpled inward door. "Let's get out of here and deal with the treason and matchmaking issues later. It sounds like the explosion completely blocked the door."

Olivia straightened and craned her neck, her gaze searching. "Something is off. I feel...something. A weird vibration."

Ronni frowned. "What do you mean?"

Olivia turned toward Helen. "Did they touch anything in the room? Leave anything?"

Helen glanced around. "I'm empathic, not psychic. I was knocked out for a little while, but I did hear them rummaging in the desk. I figured they were looking for the research I'd leaked to Olivia."

Olivia inched toward the desk and bent down to study the drawers. Gingerly, she pulled out the bottom one.

"Hell," Jared murmured, looking over her shoulder.

Olivia sucked in air. "We have a bomb, folks."

CHAPTER THIRTEEN

Chalton hurried around the desk to study the bomb. Different wires cascaded out from a compilation of material only known to the immortal world. When it blew, it'd take out the entire building.

A timer ran along the side, and he had to bend down to read it. "We have two minutes."

He levered up and glanced around the room. The outside walls were brick, the door was blocked, and the window was wired from the outside. "Everybody take cover. It has been a while, but I'll do what I can," he said evenly, trying to remain calm.

Ronni cleared her throat and stood up. "I have no clue how to diffuse a bomb." She grasped Helen's arm and drew her over to the bookshelf. "Anybody?"

"I know more than most." Chalton reached for a pair of scissors on the desk, his gaze on Olivia. "When you sense lies or truth...what is it like?"

She blinked, panic darkening her eyes. "Like?"

"Yes. Do you smell a lie? See a lie? Just sense it?"

She rapidly shook her head. "There's a subtle vibration I sense through the air."

He smiled and tried to banish all concern. "Good. That's good. Come here."

She moved without hesitation, arriving at his side and kneeling down, her gaze on the bomb. "I don't know anything about bombs."

He gripped the scissors. "Wires send out vibrations, just like people do." He leaned toward her. "I'm going to press on each wire, and I want you to listen to and catalog the sound."

She swallowed and glanced at him. "I can see patterns in books, colors, words, speech, even the air sometimes."

He frowned, wanting nothing more than to force open the door and tell her to run. "You see one here?" he asked instead.

She gulped in air and studied the bomb. "The wires. Colors and crossing." A tingling set up from her...popping the air around him. "I don't sense the bad ones."

He angled to the side, the scissors at ready. "This pink wire is an instant detonation if cut. I can tell by the way it's inserted. We have to cut all the other ones first, but I don't know the order." Careful and slow, he pressed the scissors on the wire.

She glanced up, her face pale. "Okay. That was shrill."

He hadn't heard a thing. She was amazing but obviously getting freaked out. Couldn't blame her. "Okay. Let's try the yellow one." He tried to convey confidence in his gaze.

"Not as bad," she said. "I can hear the difference."

"Good. Now blue." He went through each one, careful not to cut. Finally, they were done. "In order from barely shrill to very shrill, it goes blue, yellow, red, black, and then pink. Right?"

Tears filled her eyes. "No way will this work." She pushed back her hair, and her hand visibly shook. "The good news is that even if we blow up, you won't die, right?"

He wanted to lie to her, but she'd know it. "We can die, sweetheart. By beheading, by losing all our blood, and by being blown to bits."

She grimaced. "Oh. Guess we'd better get this right." She bent down so close she was almost nose-to-nose with the myriad of wires. Just in case this was it, she couldn't leave things unsaid. "I do love you, you know," she whispered.

"I know," he whispered back. "I realize it doesn't make sense to you, but when it happens, it happens quickly for my people. I love you, too."

She glanced up, a small smile on her face, tears in her eyes. "Guess we'd better live."

"Fucking get to it," Jared ordered from across the room where he and Theo tried to shield Ronni and Helen.

"I'm sorry we didn't talk for so long," Chalton said. There was a chance that his crazy plan wouldn't work, and he'd end up in pieces. It was time to become a strong family again, even if it was during his last moments. "You're my brothers, and I carry you with me at all times."

Theo nodded. "Ditto, and a hundred years isn't long, really. We would've caught up."

"Yeah," Jared said with a low growl. "Without anybody committing treason."

Helen sighed. "I believe we're running out of time. I love you boys."

"You can do this. Blue wire first," Olivia said quietly.

Chalton, his hand steady, clipped the blue wire.

Olivia breathed out. "Good. Okay, good. Um, twenty seconds. Yellow wire."

He moved to cut. It seemed to help her to direct, so he let her, although he'd already memorized the order.

"The red wire."

He swallowed and then snipped the red wire, his body tensing for the explosion.

Nothing.

His chest heaved. "Fifteen seconds."

She grimaced, her gaze on the wires. "The next is the black wire, but it's underneath the pink one. You can't cut the pink."

He inched to the side and slid the scissors beneath the pink wire, holding his breath. With a slight twist of his fingers, he snapped the black wire and glanced at the timer. "Ten seconds."

She coughed. "Thank you for the last couple days. They were crazy but the best of my life."

"Ditto." He snapped the pink wire, dropping the scissors and tackling her to the ground, covering her completely.

Quiet reigned.

She looked up at him, her gaze wide.

Slowly, he turned and moved back to the bomb. It had frozen at one second. One second.

"Are we done?" Jared asked, tension riding his voice.

Chalton went limp. "Yeah. Bomb's out." He yanked Olivia into him and covered her mouth with his, taking her deep and showing her everything he was feeling. She kissed him back, giving him the sense of coming home. Finally.

A throat clearing drew him away from her.

"We still need to get out of here," Jared snapped, heading for the bookcase and tossing books on the floor. "We'll have to go through the inner wall to the next office and so on until we can get out to the hallway."

Chalton nodded and moved to help pull the bookshelf away from the wall.

"Me first." Theo pivoted in a stunning spin-kick to demolish the drywall.

Olivia rushed for the hidden wall safe on the other side, opened it, and drew out her laptop and a stack of manila files.

Jared jumped in to assist Theo, and within minutes, they were in a small office that appeared to belong to a bunch of performing belly dancers, based on the costumes strewn around.

They had to attack another inner wall to enter a magician's office to be able to access the outer hallway. Once there, they filed out single-handedly the same way they'd arrived.

Sirens trilled in the distance.

"We need to be out of here," Chalton said, leading the way into the sunlight and around the corner. "Look natural." He glanced left and right, looking for a threat but finding nothing.

Crowds moved past them, several people stopping to gape at the smoke billowing out of the brick building from the inner hallway explosion. The smoke was secondary without any remaining fire, so hopefully nobody had been harmed. He couldn't smell any blood or sense death, so the strike had been localized well.

Chalk one up for Petey.

The crowd thickened, and he tried to maneuver between shopping bags and kids on a field trip holding museum bags. He paused near an alley, scouted the quiet row, and moved on.

A man in a hat jostled him, stepped by, and shoved Olivia into the alley.

Chalton turned in time to see a knife flash against her delicate skin. Everything in him quieted, and he shut off all emotion, even as he wanted to roar. He followed with his brothers flanking him, guns already out.

The hat fell off.

"Petey," Chalton breathed, his focus on the knife pressed against her vulnerable jugular. Her fear climbed into him, and he had to concentrate to keep from losing his mind. His entire body heated and then chilled to ice. Petey held her around the waist, knife to her throat, her back to his front.

"You took out my bomb?" Petey asked, his blue eyes flashing.

Standing well over six-feet tall, the blond easily pulled Olivia deeper into the alley.

"Yes." Chalton took note of the area, looking for a place to take him down. A series of stench-riddled garbage bins lined the way, while puddles glimmered all over. "Why don't you stop hiding behind a little human?"

Petey pressed his nose to her hair and breathed deeply. "Your little human. She reeks of you."

Olivia's eyes widened, fear filling the green. Her head was back and her head was arched to avoid the sharp blade digging in. A sliver of blood rolled down her neck.

Chalton fought to keep from turning into the predator living inside him. "Only cowards hide behind women." Or kidnap mothers.

Petey shrugged. "Your people killed my father. I guess killing your mate is a fair exchange."

"She's not my mate," Chalton ground out, angling a little to the right as Jared went left. "But I will avenge her death in ways you can't even imagine right now." She *was* his mate, and his fangs tried to flash. A rumbled set through him. Everything inside him rioted at the image of her in danger. "I will kill you, Petey."

"Ah. The Realm assassin makes an appearance. Thought you went limp there," Petey spat, backing away.

"Just took a vacation." It had been way too long since he'd fired a weapon, but there was only one chance to save Olivia. "Let the girl go, and I won't kill you."

Petey smiled and let his fangs drop. "No."

Allowing instinct to take over, Chalton grabbed his weapon and fired.

The bullet impacted Petey's wrist, going right through to his collarbone and missing Olivia by centimeters. Petey dropped the knife and yelled as blood sprayed from his injury.

Chalton leaped for him, shoving Olivia away and continuing down to the ground. Nothing existed. No thought, no feeling...only protecting his mate.

His knife was instantly in his hand from his boot, and he shoved down through Petey's throat right to the concrete. Grunting, Chalton twisted right and then left, sawing until the head rolled under a dumpster.

He growled and stood, wiping his knife on his jeans. Turning, his fangs out, blood on his face, he saw Olivia right before she pitched forward in a dead faint. Theo caught her before she could hit the dirty ground.

Slowly, reality returned to Chalton. His brothers and mom stared at him, concern bright in their eyes.

He focused on the woman he loved. To save her, he'd had to become what he'd vowed never to become again. A monster who killed.

Had he just lost her?

* * * *

Olivia settled into the plush sofa at Helen's house, her gaze on the slowly forming king on the broad plasma television. Apparently vampires rarely used texting and instead had to see each other in full color.

Ronni perched quietly on a settee, drinking an iced tea, more pale than ever. Helen was in the other room trying to keep Uncle Benny from sending troops to kill Chalton, while he and his brothers stood as a unit to face the television.

King Dage Kayrs stood as well, his hands behind his back. "Is it over?"

"Yes," Chalton said. "We have the research and have stopped the stories. The mission is concluded."

Dage frowned and studied Chalton. "Are you all right?"

"Fine, King. Stop worrying," Chalton said.

The king nodded, glancing to the sides. "It's good to see you and your brothers together." He focused on Jared. "He's been lonely without you."

"Ditto," Jared said.

"Good." The king visibly relaxed. "Your mother was matchmaking instead of committing treason, as far as I'm concerned. We'll keep her involvement out of any reports whatsoever, so this stays between us. The issue is concluded."

"No." Olivia sucked deep for courage and stood to face what could only be termed a deadly predator. "I haven't promised to stop writing the articles."

Dage's eyebrows rose. "Chalton? Your mate seems to have a different idea than you do."

"We haven't mated," Olivia said as sweetly as she could.

"We will," Chalton shot back.

"Maybe." She tried to appear calm and not scared shitless. "That's private, and we'll discuss it later." As of now, her insisting on accompanying him on the mission had resulted in his killing somebody, and a new darkness had entered his eyes. Did he resent her? He had a right. "My business is with the king."

"Is that so?" Chalton asked, his voice dangerously mild.

She shivered. "Yep. Here's the deal. You promised to save my friend, King. If you figure out how to do so, then I'll even write an article debunking the extra-chromosomal species." She could come up with something interesting that made sense and might still help human scientists. "Deal?"

The king studied her, his silver eyes nearly glowing. "Chalton? Any ideas?"

Ronni cleared her throat. "Um, hi, Vampire King. I'm not mating Chalton. Period."

Amusement flashed across Dage's face. "I could find you a lonely shifter."

Was he kidding? Olivia frowned.

"I'll mate her." Jared stepped closer to the camera.

Ronni gasped. "Ah, well, hmmm."

He turned to face her. "You want to live or not?"

"I really do," she murmured. "But the whole mating thing? It's forever."

"Yes," he said.

Olivia shook her head. "It doesn't have to be."

"Yet it does," Jared said, his gaze not leaving Ronni's.

Dage chuckled. "Well then, problem solved. Olivia? Send me a copy of your new article as soon as it's written. Chalton? Take all the time you need with your family, but please do check in." The king clicked off without another word.

Chalton shook his head. "Olivia? Would you and Ronni please join my mother in the other room? I'd like to talk to my brothers."

Olivia nodded and tried to keep her knees from shaking.

Ronni opened her mouth to protest, and Jared shook his head. "We'll talk in a few minutes, and I'll lay out your options for you. For now, please give us a moment."

Olivia took her hand. "Let's go." If nothing else, they could probably make a break for it.

CHAPTER FOURTEEN

Chalton waited until the door closed behind Olivia. "Have you lost your damn mind?"

"Probably." Jared crossed to the bar and poured three glasses of aged Scotch. "But here's the deal. Olivia won't stop until her friend is saved, and the king will be forced to do something about it, which would just hurt you."

"We can find her somebody else to mate," Chalton muttered.

"True, but this way, our mates will be friends and maybe we'll see more of each other." Jared handed glasses to Chalton and Theo.

Chalton drew himself up short. "I'm sorry about the last century, but you sure as shit don't need to mate my mate's friend to stay in contact."

Jared took a deep swallow and hummed in pleasure. "I know, but why not? I hadn't planned on mating, so why not save Olivia's friend? We can mate, I can save her, and then we can go our separate ways."

Chalton frowned. "Do you think it'll be that easy?"

"Sure." Jared took another drink.

Man, was he clueless.

Theo snorted and shook his head. Then he sobered. "Are you all right, Chalton? I mean, with, you know."

"Killing Petey?" Chalton tipped back his head and took a deep swallow, allowing the potent brew to warm his insides. "I think so." But he'd made Olivia faint. Would she ever be able to see him as anything but the killer he was at heart? "I might have a few more nightmares, but he was threatening my mate."

Jared nodded. "You did what you had to do."

"Amen," Theo said.

Chalton grinned. It was good being with his brothers again. "You know what this all means, right?"

Theo shook his head.

"You're both part of the Realm now, whether you like it or not." Man, it'd be fun to see Dage try to meddle in Jared's life. The king couldn't help it.

Jared snorted. "Great."

Yeah, it actually was great. Chalton nodded.

Jared shuffled his feet. "I guess it wouldn't harm us to align with the Realm. Dage was pretty cool about mom committing treason."

Chalton nodded. "He's a bigger matchmaker than mom. God help us if they ever sit down to chat."

Theo coughed. "They both can stay away from my love life. I'm not mating for centuries."

"We'll see." Chalton downed the rest of his glass and turned for the doorway. "Speaking of mates, I need to set things straight with Olivia."

Theo cleared his throat. "What if she's not okay with, well, everything? She did faint."

Chalton nodded, not stopping. "I know, and she doesn't have a choice. She will be all right." He hoped that was true. The idea of losing her now hurt somewhere deeper than his body.

He steeled his shoulders, strode into the kitchen, and tossed her over his shoulder.

She gave a small eek and tried to find her balance.

He grinned. They might as well get things off to the right start. Planting his hand across her ass, he easily kept her in place.

* * * *

What in the world was happening? Once again, she was upside down over his massive shoulder. "Damn it, Chalton." She punched him in the kidney. "You have got to stop doing this." She'd been in the middle of a discussion with Helen about real events at the turn of the century.

"No." His strides were relaxed and easy as they wound through several hallways to enter a bedroom decorated with a nautical theme. He bent over, and she ended up sitting on a bed. "We need to talk."

Her heart hurt. "Are you mad at me?"

He frowned and crossed his muscled arms. "No. Are you afraid of me?"

"No." She licked her lips. "Sorry about the whole fainting thing. I missed breakfast." And had never been held at knifepoint or seen a fight to the death.

He grinned. "You're going to mate me."

Yeah, she was. "Well. You might have to court me first, and meet my grandfather." And tell her all about his hundreds of years of life. Maybe she should write a fictional novel about his times. Yeah.

"I can do that." He leaned over her and brushed his lips against hers.

"We have plenty of time to court." What a nice, old-fashioned word.

He leaned back, his face an inch away from hers, his dark eyes blazing. "Not really. I'll give you a week, but you're wearing my bite at that point."

She breathed in. "Wait a minute."

"I will. An entire week."

It was going to take her a lot longer than a week to tame his Neanderthal tendencies. She might as well do it while being immortal. "A week it is." She smiled.

Possessiveness and promise glittered in his masculine gaze. "I love you, Olivia."

She wrapped both arms around his neck. "I love you more."

"Impossible." Then he kissed her, filling her with what could only be love and hope for the future. The very long future.

Sign up for the 1001 Dark Nights Newsletter
and be entered to win a Tiffany Key necklace.

There's a contest every month!

Go to www.1001DarkNights.com to subscribe.

As a bonus, all subscribers will receive a free
1001 Dark Nights story
The First Night
by Lexi Blake & M.J. Rose

Turn the page for a full list of the
1001 Dark Nights fabulous novellas...

1001 DARK NIGHTS

WICKED WOLF by Carrie Ann Ryan
A Redwood Pack Novella

WHEN IRISH EYES ARE HAUNTING by Heather Graham
A Krewe of Hunters Novella

EASY WITH YOU by Kristen Proby
A With Me In Seattle Novella

MASTER OF FREEDOM by Cherise Sinclair
A Mountain Masters Novella

CARESS OF PLEASURE by Julie Kenner
A Dark Pleasures Novella

ADORED by Lexi Blake
A Masters and Mercenaries Novella

HADES by Larissa Ione
A Demonica Novella

RAVAGED by Elisabeth Naughton
An Eternal Guardians Novella

DREAM OF YOU by Jennifer L. Armentrout
A Wait For You Novella

STRIPPED DOWN by Lorelei James
A Blacktop Cowboys ® Novella

RAGE/KILLIAN by Alexandra Ivy/Laura Wright
Bayou Heat Novellas

DRAGON KING by Donna Grant
A Dark Kings Novella

PURE WICKED by Shayla Black
A Wicked Lovers Novella

HARD AS STEEL by Laura Kaye
A Hard Ink/Raven Riders Crossover

STROKE OF MIDNIGHT by Lara Adrian
A Midnight Breed Novella

ALL HALLOWS EVE by Heather Graham
A Krewe of Hunters Novella

KISS THE FLAME by Christopher Rice
A Desire Exchange Novella

DARING HER LOVE by Melissa Foster
A Bradens Novella

TEASED by Rebecca Zanetti
A Dark Protectors Novella

THE PROMISE OF SURRENDER by Liliana Hart
A MacKenzie Family Novella

FOREVER WICKED by Shayla Black
A Wicked Lovers Novella

CRIMSON TWILIGHT by Heather Graham
A Krewe of Hunters Novella

CAPTURED IN SURRENDER by Liliana Hart
A MacKenzie Family Novella

SILENT BITE: A SCANGUARDS WEDDING by Tina Folsom
A Scanguards Vampire Novella

DUNGEON GAMES by Lexi Blake
A Masters and Mercenaries Novella

AZAGOTH by Larissa Ione
A Demonica Novella

NEED YOU NOW by Lisa Renee Jones
A Shattered Promises Series Prelude

SHOW ME, BABY by Cherise Sinclair
A Masters of the Shadowlands Novella

ROPED IN by Lorelei James
A Blacktop Cowboys ® Novella

TEMPTED BY MIDNIGHT by Lara Adrian
A Midnight Breed Novella

THE FLAME by Christopher Rice
A Desire Exchange Novella

CARESS OF DARKNESS by Julie Kenner
A Dark Pleasures Novella

Also from Evil Eye Concepts:

TAME ME by J. Kenner
A Stark International Novella

THE SURRENDER GATE By Christopher Rice
A Desire Exchange Novel

SERVICING THE TARGET By Cherise Sinclair
A Masters of the Shadowlands Novel

ABOUT REBECCA ZANETTI

Rebecca Zanetti is the author of over twenty-five dark paranormals, romantic suspense, and contemporary romances, and her books have appeared multiple times on the New York Times, USA Today, and Amazon bestseller lists. She has received a Publisher's Weekly Starred Review for Wicked Edge, Romantic Times Reviewer Choice Nominations for Forgotten Sins and Sweet Revenge, and RT Top Picks for several of her novels. She believes strongly in luck, karma, and working her butt off...and she thinks one of the best things about being an author, unlike the lawyer she used to be, is that she can let the crazy out. Her current series are: The Scorpius Syndrome, The Dark Protectors, The Realm Enforcers, The Sin Brothers, and The Lost Bastards. Find Rebecca at: www.rebeccazanetti.com

TRICKED

A Dark Protectors Novella
By Rebecca Zanetti
Coming October 25, 2016

He Might Save Her

Former police psychologist Ronni Alexander had it all before a poison attacked her heart and gave her a death sentence. Now, on her last leg, she has an opportunity to live if she mates a vampire. A real vampire. One night of sex and a good bite, and she'd live forever with no more weaknesses. Well, except for the vampire whose dominance is over the top, and who has no clue how to deal with a modern woman who can take care of herself.

She Might Kill Him

Jared Reese, who has no intention of ever mating for anything other than convenience, agrees to help out his new sister in law by saving her friend's life with a quick tussle in bed. The plan seems so simple. They'd mate, and he move on with his life and take risks as a modern pirate should. Except after one night with Ronni, one moment of her sighing his name, and he wants more than a mating of convenience. Now all he has to do is convince Ronni she wants the same thing. Good thing he's up for a good battle.

MERCURY STRIKING

By Rebecca Zanetti

Book #1 of The Scorpius Syndrome series

Coming January 26, 2016

With nothing but rumors to lead her, Lynn Harmony has trekked across a nightmare landscape to find one man—a mysterious, damaged legend who protects the weak and leads the strong. He's more than muscle and firepower—and in post-plague L.A., he's her only hope. As the one woman who could cure the disease, Lynn is the single most volatile—and vulnerable—creature in this new and ruthless world. But face to face with Jax Mercury...

Danger has never looked quite so delicious...

"Thrilling post-apocalyptic romance at its dark, sizzling best!" —Lara Adrian

"Nothing is easy or black or white in Zanetti's grim new reality, but hope is key, and I *hope* she writes faster!" —*New York Times* bestselling author Larissa Ione

* * * *

MERCURY STRIKING

In the end, there is no doubt that Mother Nature will win.
--Dr. Frank. X Harmony, *Philosophies*

CHAPTER ONE

Life on Earth is at the ever-increasing risk of being wiped out by a disaster, such as sudden global warming, nuclear war, a genetically engineered virus, or other dangers we have not yet thought of.
--Stephen Hawking

Despair hungered in the darkness, not lingering, not languishing . . . but waiting to bite. No longer the little brother of rage, despair had taken over the night, ever present, an actor instead of an afterthought.

Lynne picked her way along the deserted twelve-lane interstate, allowing the weak light from the moon to guide her. An unnatural silence hung heavy over the barren land. Rusting carcasses of vehicles lined the sides; otherwise, the once-vibrant 405 was dead.

Her months of hiding had taught her stealth. Prey needed stealth, as did the hunter.

She was both.

The tennis shoes she'd stolen from an abandoned thrift store protected her feet from the cracked asphalt, while a breeze scented with death and decomposing vegetation lifted her hair. The smell had saturated the wind as she'd trekked across the country.

The world was littered with dead bodies and devoid of souls.

A click echoed in the darkness. About time. Predators, both human and animal, crouched in every shadow, but she'd made it closer to what used to be Los Angeles than she'd hoped.

A strobe light hit her full on, rendering sight impossible. The miracle of functioning batteries brought pain. She closed her eyes. They'd either kill her or not. Either way, no need to go blind. "I want to see Mercury." Since she'd aimed for the center of Mercury's known territory, hopefully she'd find him and not some rogue gang.

Silence. Then several more clicks. Guns of some type. They'd closed in silently, just as well trained as she'd heard. As she'd hoped.

She forced strength into her voice. "You don't want to kill me without taking me to Mercury first." Jax Mercury, to be exact. If he still lived. If not, she was screwed anyway.

"Why would we do that?" A voice from the darkness, angry and near.

She squinted, blinking until her pupils narrowed. The bright light exposed her and concealed them, weakening her knees, but she gently set her small backpack on the ground. She had to clear her throat to force out sound. "I'm Lynne Harmony."

Gasps, low and male, filled the abyss around her. "Bullshit," a voice hissed from her left.

She tilted her head toward the voice, and then slowly, so slowly they wouldn't be spooked, she unbuttoned her shirt. No catcalls, no suggestive responses followed. Shrugging her shoulders, she dropped the cotton to the ground, facing the light.

She hadn't worn a bra, but she doubted the echoing exhales of shock were from her size Bs. More likely the shimmering blue outline of her heart caught their attention. Yeah, she was a freak. Typhoid Mary in the body of a woman who'd failed. Big time. But she might be able to save the men surrounding her. "So. Jax Mercury. Now."

One man stepped closer. Gang tattoos lined his face, inked tears showing his kills. He might have been thirty, he might have been sixty. Regardless, he was dangerous, and he smelled like dust combined with body odor. A common smell in the plague-riddled world. Eyeing her chest, he quickly crossed himself. "Holy Mary, Mother of God."

"Not even close." A silent overpass loomed a few yards to the north, and her voice echoed off the concrete. The piercing light assaulted her, spinning the background thick and dark. Her temples pounded, and her hollow stomach ached. Wearily, she reached down and grabbed her shirt, shrugging it back on. She figured the "take me to your leader" line would get her shot. "Do you want to live or not?"

He met her gaze, his scarred upper lip twisting. "Yes."

It was the most sincere sound she'd heard in months. "We're running out of time." Time had deserted them long ago, but she needed to get a move on. "Please." The sound shocked her, the civility of it, a word she'd forgotten how to use. The slightest of hopes warmed that blue organ in her chest, reminding her of who she used to be. Who she'd lost.

Another figure stepped forward, this one big and silent. Deadly power vibrated in the shift of muscle as light illuminated him from behind, shrouding his features. "I didn't tell you to put your shirt back on." No emotion, no hint of humanity echoed in the deep rumble.

His lack of emotion twittered anxiety through her empty abdomen. Without missing a beat, she secured each button, keeping the movements slow and sure. "I take it you're Mercury." Regardless of name, there was no doubt the guy was in charge.

"If I am?" Soft, his voice promised death.

A promise she'd make him keep. Someday. The breeze picked up, tumbling weeds across the lonely 405 to halt against a Buick stripped to its rims. She quelled a shiver. Any weakness shown might get her killed. "You know who I am," she whispered.

"I know who you say you are." His overwhelming form blocked out the light, reminding her of her smaller size. "Take off your shirt."

Something about his command gave her pause. Before, she hadn't cared. But with him so close she could smell *male*, an awareness of her femininity brought fresh fear. Nevertheless, she again unbuttoned her shirt.

This time, her hands trembled.

Straightening her spine, she squared her shoulders and left the shirt on, the worn material gaping in front.

He waited.

She lifted her chin, trying to meet his eyes although she couldn't see them. The men around them remained silent, yet alertness carried on the oxygen. How many guns were trained on her? She wanted to tell them it would only take one. Though she'd been through hell, she'd never really learned to fight.

The wind whipped into action, lifting her long hair away from her face. Her arms tightened against her rib cage. Goose bumps rose over her skin. She was accustomed to being vulnerable, and she was used to feeling alone. But she'd learned to skirt danger.

There was no doubt the man in front of her was *all* danger.

She shivered again.

Swearing quietly, he stepped in, long, tapered fingers drawing her shirt apart. He shifted to the side, allowing light to blast her front. Neon blue glowed along her flesh.

"Jesus." He pressed his palm against her breastbone—directly above her heart.

Shock tightened her muscles, and that heart ripped into a gallop. Her nipples pebbled from the breeze. Warmth cascaded from his hand when he spread his fingers over the odd blue of her skin, easily spanning her upper chest. When was the last time someone had touched her gently?

And gentle, he was.

The contact had her looking down at his damaged hand. Faded white scars slashed across his knuckles, above the veins, past his wrist. The bizarre glow from her heart filtered through his fingers. Her entire chest was aqua from within, those veins closest to her heart, which glowed neon blue, shining strong enough to be seen through her ribs and sternum.

He exhaled softly, removing his touch.

An odd sense of loss filtered down her spine. Then surprise came as he quickly buttoned her shirt to the top.

He clasped her by the elbow. "Cut the light." His voice didn't rise, but instantly, the light was extinguished. "I'm Mercury. What do you want?"

What a question. What she wanted, nobody could provide. Yet she struggled to find the right words. Night after night, fleeing under darkness to reach him, she'd planned for this moment. But the words wouldn't come. She wanted to breathe. To rest. To hide. "Help. I need your help." The truth tumbled out too fast to stop.

He stiffened and tightened his hold. "That, darlin', you're gonna have to earn."

Welcome to Storm, Texas, where passion runs hot, desire runs deep, and secrets have the power to destroy...

Nestled among rolling hills and painted with vibrant wildflowers, the bucolic town of Storm, Texas, seems like nothing short of perfection.

But there are secrets beneath the facade. Dark secrets. Powerful secrets. The kind that can destroy lives and tear families apart. The kind that can cut through a town like a tempest, leaving jealousy and destruction in its wake, along with shattered hopes and broken dreams. All it takes is one little thing to shatter that polish.

Reading like an on-going drama in the tradition of classic day and night-time soap operas like Dallas, Dynasty, and All My Children, *Rising Storm* is full of scandal, deceit, romance, passion, and secrets.

With 1001 Dark Nights as the "producer," Julie Kenner and Dee Davis use a television model with each week building on the last to create a storyline that fulfills the promise of a drama-filled soap opera. Joining Kenner and Davis in the "writer's room" is an incredible group of *New York Times* bestselling authors such as Lexi Blake, Elisabeth Naughton, Jennifer Probst, Larissa Ione, Rebecca Zanetti and Lisa Mondello who have brought their vision of Storm to life.

A serial soap opera containing eight episodes in season one, the season premiere of *Rising Storm*, TEMPEST RISING, debuted September 24th with each subsequent episode released consecutively that fall.

So get ready. The storm is coming.

Experience Rising Storm Here… http://risingstormbooks.com

On behalf of 1001 Dark Nights,
Liz Berry and M.J. Rose would like to thank ~

Steve Berry
Doug Scofield
Kim Guidroz
Jillian Stein
InkSlinger PR
Dan Slater
Asha Hossain
Chris Graham
Pamela Jamison
Jessica Johns
Dylan Stockton
Richard Blake
BookTrib After Dark
The Dinner Party Show
and Simon Lipskar

Printed in Poland
by Amazon Fulfillment
Poland Sp. z o.o., Wrocław